DARK MEMORY

To: My "Favorite
Ex-Coworker"
Spencer,

Don't know if you'll
enjoy this. I wrote
this when I was
thirteen. This is so
embarassing. ~~embarassing~~ Have fun!

)

— Delsy
and in case I get
famous....

all my signatures... might
be worth something someday...
hopefully

DARK MEMORY

Delsy Gonzalez

iUniverse, Inc.
New York Lincoln Shanghai

Dark Memory

iUniverse, Inc.

For information address:
iUniverse, Inc.
2021 Pine Lake Road, Suite 100
Lincoln, NE 68512
www.iuniverse.com

ISBN: 0-595-27202-9

Printed in the United States of America

CHAPTER 1

IT WAS A DARK AND COOL NIGHT. THE WIND WHISTLED THROUGH THE TREES. THE bright full moon was the only light in the darkness of the night. It was very silent. No one was around and not even the crickets were chirping. There was just plain silence.

A mysterious man strolled through the night. He was the only one outside at that time. He usually wore a dark hood over his head to conceal his identity, but it was so dark so he thought that there was no need to.

The man walked over to the only house that had a light on. He knocked very lightly on the door. A woman answered it. She was in her nightgown. She did not expect anyone to be knocking on her door that late at night. "Umm…hello," she greeted the man questioningly.

"How are you tonight, ma'am?" the man asked politely. He did not wait for an answer; he just kept on speaking. "I need to inspect your home."

A young man that lived across the street from the woman saw the strange man at her house. He stepped out of his house quietly and began to watch everything that was happening.

"Why do you need to inspect my home?" the woman asked. "I don't even know who you are."

"You don't need to know who I am. I need to inspect your home because there is a killer that creeps into people's homes and waits until they go to bed to kill them. This killer is very dangerous and you need to be aware of these things."

"Okay," the woman said with hesitation. "Come on in."

The man entered the house and began to look around it. He searched every hiding place possible.

The young man across the street was confused. He was wondering why the woman would let a stranger into her home. No one had ever seen that man anywhere. He was just hoping that nothing would go wrong. In case of anything, he stayed outside and watched her house.

The woman stood there and watched the strange man investigate her house. "No sign of him yet?" she asked.

The man stopped searching and looked at her. "No," he answered. "You are free from harm. The killer is not in your house." He looked over at a red drink that was on a table. "What is that?"

The woman looked at what he was looking at. She answered, "That's my invention. It's a type of fruit punch. It's really good. Do you want to try some?"

"Sure," answered the man. While the woman went into her kitchen to serve him a drink, he took a small vial of liquid out of his dark coat and opened it up. He poured it inside the drink that was on the table and then put the vial back inside his coat.

The woman came back with the drink. "Here you go," she said.

The man took the drink from her. "Thank you," he told her. "You are very kind." He took a sip from the drink. "This is quite delicious. You're good at inventing drinks."

The woman got a hold of her drink. "Thank you." She began to drink out of the cup.

The man stopped drinking the beverage and watched the woman drink hers. He watched her finish her drink. The woman looked at him. "Sir, aren't you going to finish…?" She was not able to finish the question. She collapsed to the floor immediately.

The man smiled vilely and put his drink on the table. He then stepped over the woman and looked down at her. "Have a nice night, ma'am," he said. After that he left the house and began to walk down the street.

The young man across the street watched him leave. Shortly he looked at the house that was across the street from his. He saw that the door was still wide open. He wondered why the woman did not close it. He decided to go over there and find out what was going on.

The young man arrived there and saw the woman on the floor. He quickly kneeled down beside her and checked her pulse. She had no pulse for she was dead.

"No," the young man angrily said almost in a whisper. "That bastard did this to her."

The young man decided not to inform the police because he did not think that the mysterious man would ever come around again.

The bright sun was glaring down at the city below with its fierce rays. People were walking here and there and many of them had to use umbrellas because of the greatness of the heat. The sounds of traffic roaring were what made the city very noisy.

In that city was a busy police station. The city was quite poor and it was not able to afford to pay officers and detectives separately; so policemen had to do the same jobs as detectives at the station.

The chief of the station had two sons that were excellent officers there. The older one was Will. He was a tall and slim man with a tenacious attitude. He would always stick to what he usually thought was best. It was very hard to convince him otherwise. Jon was the other son of the chief. He was somewhat diminutive for a man and he was neither thin nor plump. He had a kind and brave heart and was close to being the opposite of his brother. If someone gave him a good reason for something, it would easily convince him, but he was not gullible.

Jon slammed a piece of paper that he had finished reading onto a desk. "Look at this," he said to his brother. He stood up from his chair and looked down at the paper. Will paid very close attention to him. He always did. He was a very good listener. "This is the third murder this week. That killer brutally stabbed a man to death. We have to catch this killer already. He's been on our *Most Wanted* lists for months. We can't even get a description of him because we don't know what he looks like. How are we ever going to stop this guy?"

Will answered Jon's question in a question. "Haven't you noticed that he always commits his murders at night? If we're around at night, then maybe we can see him strolling around somewhere."

Jon looked up from the paper that he was staring at. "I know we're going to catch him somehow." That was the way he was—very brave and always ready for anything. He had been a police officer for three years, solved many crimes, and caught about thirty criminals. That was actually plenty of criminals since they were so elusive—especially the one that was being spoken about.

Will looked at the clock that was on the desk. "Look what time it is," he said. "Our time here is over. Let's finally go home."

Jon stayed silent for a moment as Will began to put things away. He organized a few papers and then faced his brother. "We'll continue this case tomorrow."

Jon turned toward the door and said, "Let's tell dad that we're going home." He went out the door. Will followed him. They went down a small hallway and into a room at the end of it.

The chief of police was sitting at his desk. He was about the same size as Jon and a little bit overweight. He had a doughnut in his left hand and a pen in the other. He was writing something. He looked up when he heard his two sons enter his office. He asked, "You two are leaving already?"

"Yes," Jon replied. "We just wanted to let you know."

"Okay. I'll probably see you around midnight or so."

"Okay. Goodbye, dad."

They bid their farewells to each other. Before they went out the door, the chief said, "Will, hold on."

Will turned around and faced his father.

"Remember that you have to work overtime tomorrow. Don't go home at the regular time."

"Yes, I remembered that." Will went over to his father's desk and grabbed a doughnut. "I just feel like eating one of these right now." Then he and Jon went out the door.

While Will and Jon were walking toward their police cruiser, Jon said, "I have to get that dog trained sooner or later. He's almost a year old already."

Will took a bite out of the doughnut. "You don't have to rush," he said with his mouth full. He swallowed what he had in his mouth. "That dog is smart. It's a German Shepherd. You could wait another two years if you wanted to." He took another bite out of the doughnut.

"But I don't want to. We need a dog as soon as possible to help us solve our crimes. It'll be faster and easier."

Will took the last bite out of the doughnut and grabbed the key that belonged to the door of the car. "We've solved many crimes on our own. Why are you saying that we need a dog?" He unlocked the passenger door. Then he walked around the car and opened the driver's door. He stepped into the car and shut the door.

Jon closed his door. "I have to feed him as soon as we get home. He must be starving."

Will started up the car. He backed up and drove out of the parking lot. "You worry so much about that dog," he mentioned. "You worry so much about everything. You're like almost paranoid."

"No, I'm not," Jon answered as he looked out the window. "I know that things are good but I just want them better." He watched as two people in a car were arguing. It was simple to tell because they kept on yelling loudly. It could be heard. The words could not be made out though. All that was heard was loud noise coming out of their mouths.

Soon Jon was not able to hear or see the people arguing because the car made a right turn. "That's one of the things that make people kill each other," he finally said.

"What?" Will asked as he stopped at a stoplight.

"These two people were arguing. I mean, it didn't look like a normal argument—they were screaming with lots of fury. They'll probably go up in rage and one of them will draw a weapon."

Will made a left turn. "That's the way things are settled these days."

"I always wonder why. Why do things have to end up in violence? I mean, if you kill someone over an argument means that you're stupid and afraid of that person because you had nothing else better to do. You just want to get rid of the person. You get what I mean?"

"Yep," Will answered as he stopped at another stoplight.

Jon stayed silent. He decided not to speak anymore the entire way. He just stared out the window and saw cows grazing in the fields. He watched as they were swiping away pests with their tails. He let out a sigh.

Will glanced over at Jon and then looked back at the road. He thought that his brother cared too much and that was his only problem. He always had a different perspective. That was what made them both different.

The cruiser parked in the driveway of the house. Will turned the engine off and took the key out of the ignition. He opened the door, stepped out of the car, and closed the door. He made sure that it was locked.

Jon, on the other hand, stayed inside the car for a moment. He looked through the crystal clear windshield. It was so clean. It was not dusty like how most cars had it. It was nearly perfect.

Jon finally stepped out of the car. He closed the door and walked over to the front doorstep. He stepped inside the house since the door was already opened. He closed it behind him.

Will shouted from the hallway. "I'm going in the shower."

Jon did not say anything. He opened the backdoor and whistled for his dog. The dog came running to him. It panted and wagged its tail frantically. It was a beautiful dog. It had a nice black and brownish coat with smooth fur. Its tail was soft and bushy. It had a fine face with attractive hazel eyes. The dog was great to have around.

Jon sat down on a step and ran his fingers through the dog's soft fur. He did not even look at the dog. He looked straight ahead of him at the yard. He said, "I'm going to get you trained as soon as possible. You're going to help us find that killer. I know you will." He looked the dog in the eye.

"Right? I think so."

Jon stood up. "I have to feed you now." He went inside the patio and grabbed the bag of dog food that was nearby. He unrolled the bag and searched for the dog's bowl. He found it and slid it over to his right side. After that he poured the dog food into the bowl and then rolled the bag back up. The dog came over and began to eat the food insatiably as if it had not been fed in days.

Jon put the bag of food back in its place and entered the house. He slowly walked past the kitchen and into the living room. He went down the hallway and into his bedroom. From there he could hear the water spraying down in the bathroom since his room was right next to it.

Jon took his belt off and threw it on his bed. He removed his handgun and put it on top of a shelf. He sat on his bed and took his shoes off. He left them on the floor in front of his bed.

Suddenly Jon did not hear the water spraying down in the bathroom anymore. He stood up and walked over to his closet. He opened the door and pulled out a towel. He threw it over his shoulder. He waited until his brother came out of the bathroom.

Minutes later Jon heard the bathroom door open. Through the doorway he saw Will standing in front of the bathroom with light blue jean shorts on that passed his knees and he was shirtless. He had a towel wrapped around the back of his neck and it hung over his shoulders. His hair was dripping wet and the droplets of water dripping down his thin torso could be clearly seen.

Will said, "I think the hot water's running out."

Jon did not say anything. It was not unusual for the hot water to be running out because that was the only thing that Will took a shower with. Every time he took a shower, steam filled the bathroom.

Jon was already accustomed to taking a shower with cold water. He entered the restroom after Will stepped out of the doorway. He closed the door behind him. He hung his towel on the hook that was on the door. Then he disrobed himself and entered the bathtub. He turned on the cold water and let it spray against his body.

Jon thought that that was a very refreshing feeling. It felt a lot better than being in the dry and humid weather. It left a strange feeling on his skin. He washed his dark hair completely and rinsed it out thoroughly. He thought that it needed to be washed again so he went along and repeated that.

After the ten-minute shower, Jon turned the water off and stepped out of the bathtub. He grabbed his towel and dried himself. He put a white shirt on and a pair of black pants. He dried his face and put the towel over his shoulder. Then he opened the door and stepped out of the bathroom.

Jon went inside his room and placed his used police uniform into the unclean laundry. He hung his towel up on his room door to dry. He then lied down in his comfortable bed. He needed a good rest.

Jon heard Will's keys clashing against each other. He knew that he was going somewhere.

Will shouted, "I'm going somewhere. I'll see you soon."

Jon stayed silent. He later heard the door open and slam shut. The next thing he heard was an automobile start up and drive away.

Jon just lied there in his bed. He did not even move. He was lying on his side. Eventually he fell into deep sleep.

It felt as if Jon had been sleeping for five minutes. When he opened his eyes, he saw that everything was pitch-black. He wondered how long he had been sleeping. He looked at the glowing clock that was sitting on his counter—it was half past eleven. He had been sleeping for five hours.

Jon stepped out of bed and walked barefoot through the hallway. It was not totally dark anymore. There was some light from the moon coming in through the windows.

Jon went over to the kitchen and opened the refrigerator door to get a glass of water. He took the gallon out and poured water into a glass cup. He put the gallon back inside and closed the door. Then he began to drink the clear liquid.

Suddenly Jon heard a loud noise outside as if someone was trying to come in through the door. He quickly put the glass cup down and left the kitchen. He did not know who the person outside could have been. The noise just continued.

Jon stood there for a moment. He was about to go inside his bedroom and grab his weapon.

That was when the door opened and Will stepped in. He squinted through the darkness and saw his brother. "What are you doing still awake?" he questioned.

Jon let out a breath. "It's just you," he said, relieved.

"Who'd you think I was?"

"That killer that we can't catch."

Will closed the door and snickered quietly. "I told you that you were paranoid."

"I'm not. I just think that the killer can go into any house at this time. I thought you were him."

Will nodded slowly. "Okay," he started. "If you're not paranoid, then you'll be able to do what I am about to tell you. Grab your sleeping bag and sleep outside in front of the doorstep."

Jon did not respond.

"It's not like he'll come to this specific neighborhood out of all of them out there."

Jon still did not say anything.

Will realized that his brother was not going to sleep outside. "I'm going to sleep. It's going to be a big day. See you in the morning."

"Okay," Jon said.

When Will walked down the hallway and into his bedroom, Jon thought things over. He thought about what his brother just said to him. Was he really paranoid?

Jon placed that thought out of his head and went into his bedroom. He lied down on his bed. He knew that he would not be able to fall asleep. He just lied there and stared at the clock change every minute.

Jon heard Will saying that it was time to get out of bed. He slowly opened his eyes and saw that there was sunlight shining through the curtains. He did not even know he fell asleep.

Jon slowly stood up from his bed and prepared himself for work.

When the officers were ready for another big day at the station, Jon said, "I'm taking the dog today."

Will did not say anything.

Jon opened the backdoor. He stepped outside and grabbed a leash. The dog came running to him with its tail wagging. It was always content to see him.

Jon hooked the leash unto the dog's collar and brought him inside the house. He closed the door and said, "Okay, let's go."

Will opened the front door. Jon went through the doorway with the dog and then closed it and made sure that it was locked. He walked over to the cruiser and opened the back door since Will had unlocked it beforehand. He placed the dog in the backseat and shut the door. Then he entered the car himself.

Will was already in the car. He started it up, backed out of the driveway, and drove off to the police station.

When the brothers arrived at the station, Jon decided to leave the dog beside the entrance. He tied it up to a tree that was nearby. He then entered the building.

The first thing that Will and Jon did when they arrived at their job was greet their father. They walked over to his office and knocked on the door. The chief of the police said that they were able to come inside. They stepped inside and saw their father standing by his desk, speaking to a woman dressed in the police uniform. She had red hair that reached the middle of her back and green eyes. Her stature was normal and so was her weight.

"Hello, dad," Will said.

The three of them exchanged their greetings.

The chief of police then gestured toward the woman and said, "This is rookie Officer Lane. She applied for the job a couple of months ago and I thought that she would make an excellent policewoman. She completed her training greatly. She has the same schedule as the two of you and I want both of you to go step-by-step with her." He gestured toward his sons. "These are my sons, Will and Jon."

"Hello," the woman said demurely.

The two men greeted her back.

"These two are excellent officers," the chief complimented. "They will transform you into a strong and courageous policewoman." He looked at his sons. "Go ahead and show her around now. I'll see you later."

The woman walked over to the brothers and Jon opened the door for her. The three of them then left the office. The chief sat down and continued with his work.

While the three of them were walking, Will asked the woman, "So what's your first name?"

"Susan," answered she.

"I'm Will and he's Jon. We've been here for quite a while already. Are you new in town?"

"Well, my family and I moved here about five months ago. I'm a little used to it. It takes me a while to get completely settled in one place."

"I see," Will said.

The two officers began to walk Susan through many things. They told her how certain situations were handled and many tips for specific cases.

Soon it was Jon and Susan's lunch break. Jon decided to go ask Susan to join him in his break. He walked up to her and asked, "Do you want to go to the café for a quick drink of coffee?"

"Sure," replied Susan.

The two of them went to a café that was located across the street from the station. They sat outside at a small and round table. A man immediately walked up to them and asked, "May I help you?"

"I would like a cup of coffee please," Jon answered.

Susan said that she wanted the same thing.

"Coming right up," the man said.

"So what made you apply for the job?" questioned Jon.

Susan replied, "Lots of people told me that I was very risk-taking and could associate with people well. Then someone suggested that I become an officer. I liked the idea and I tried it out."

The waiter dropped off the cups of coffee on the table.

"Thanks," Jon said. He continued to talk as the waiter walked away. "That's kind of what happened to me. It was just a coincidence that my brother and I applied for the same job. We didn't know we were both going to become policemen. That's a long story, so I won't really get started on it."

Susan took a sip from the mug. Then she asked, "You're Jon, right?"

"Yeah. You wouldn't get confused between my brother and I after you really get to know us better. We're both totally different."

"Really?'

"Yeah. We barely speak to each other unless it's really necessary. It's like getting a snake and a cat to speak to each other. They won't because they both think differently."

"Are you really that distinct from one another?"

"Yes, we are." He took a drink from the coffee.

"So does that mean that he's like a rude guy if he's the opposite of you because you seem like a nice person."

"No, not necessarily," Jon answered as he put the mug down. "He has his ways of being nice to people. He's just very…How can I put it? He's very persistent."

"Seriously?"

"Yes. It's very hard to convince him to do anything or to believe anything. He'll always want to go his way. That's the way he's always been."

Soon the two of them finished their coffee and Jon paid for it. They then went back to the station.

Hours later, it was time for Jon to leave. He began to speak to his brother. "I'm leaving now," he informed him.

"Who's taking the car this time?" asked Will.

"You take the car. I can catch a bus."

"You sure?"

"Yeah." He was about to leave but he stopped and turned to Will. "I'm leaving the dog here by the way. I can't take him on the bus."

"Okay then. I'll take him home."

"Thanks." He then left.

It was midnight. The German Shepherd that had been standing outside the police station for hours sensed something in the distance that did not please him. He started to bark. He wanted to run but the chain would tighten around his neck. He continued to bark incessantly.

That was when Will stepped out of the building while speaking with Susan. "I just can't believe that…" He stopped shortly and faced the dog. "Hey, quiet down. You can't be loud now. You don't want to attract anyone's attention toward here. It's not the right time for that."

The dog began to whimper now. He still tried to free himself from the chain.

"That dog always picks the wrong time to start making noise," Will said. "That's why I always tell Jon that he wouldn't be a good police dog."

"He *is* fit to be in the K-9 unit," Susan told him.

"I don't know. I still don't think that he is. It's not my dog anyway, so I don't care."

"Well, I'll see you tomorrow. It's been nice meeting you."

"Okay. So long."

As soon as Susan walked away, Will turned to the dog and asked, "What's the matter with you? Why are you barking so late? You haven't made a noise until now." He kneeled down next to the animal and tried to calm it down and quiet it from whimpering so much.

In the distance, almost where the dog sensed the thing that he did not like, the chief was putting some old supplies away in a small room. While he was doing the task, he heard the door slam shut. He turned to see someone that he had always wanted to capture.

It was the killer. He was dressed in a dark coat with a hood over his head that covered most of his face. The only parts that were visible were his lips and chin. He had dark pants and also a pair of dark gloves and boots.

"It's you," the chief said. He was about to get ready to inform some officers that were still at the station, but he noticed that he did not have his walkie-talkie. He was going to shout for them.

"No, no, no," the killer said. "No one can hear you from here. The only way to tell them is to leave out the door, but I won't let you."

"What are you going to do—shoot me to death?"

"No. Guns are nothing but useless machines. I can't see why many people use guns. I like to be guilty for the murder, but if I use a gun, I won't be. The gun is usually the murderer. All the killer does is pull the trigger. He may not even want to kill a person. He can just pull the trigger by accident and it'll kill someone. It's the gun that killed the person.

"I don't know why people can't just kill with their bare hands. They need a manmade machine to do it for them. That is just pitiful. They have nothing better to do. That is called cheating. That means that they are foolish wimps. You are not showing courage by using a machine. So I will kill you with my bare hands."

The chief of police groped down on the side of his pants for his gun, but he could not feel it. He then quickly looked down and saw it. When he looked back up, the killer was gone. "Did he leave?" he asked.

The chief was about to head for the door, but he felt an arm wrap around his neck. The killer was choking him. "I should have never spoken so much," he said. "I'll make this murder quick and easy for you." That is when he pulled his arm back and broke the chief's neck. The lifeless chief fell onto the ground.

The killer kneeled down beside him and looked to see what was inside his pockets. He found an information paper that had the chief's signature at the bottom.

Suddenly the killer heard a dog barking furiously in the distance. He extemporaneously and quickly folded the paper and placed it in his left pocket. He opened the door and rushed out, but his coat got stuck in between the closed door and the doorway. He ripped it out and began to run off.

The German Shepherd continued to bark loudly. "What is the matter with you?" Will asked. He saw that the dog was facing a specific direction, so he looked up to see what was there. He then saw the mysterious being running off in the distance.

Will immediately broke into a run. He stopped as soon as he saw the killer disappear in the darkness. He was about to get the dog to sniff the tracks of the killer, but he turned to his side and saw the small room that the killer escaped out of. He opened the door and saw a ripped piece of cloth on the floor. He picked it up. "He was here," he said. "Why?"

When Will looked up, he saw his father lying on the floor. "What the hell?" he exclaimed as he rushed over to the chief. He kneeled down and realized that his father was dead. "That damned bastard did this." He slammed his fist on the floor. "I'm going to kill him!" He was so dejected about his father's death that he forgot about following the killer's tracks. He promised himself that he would find him.

The next day arrived. The news of the chief's murder spread around very quickly. Since it was caught on a surveillance camera, the officers watched what happened. They were not able to believe what they saw.

After all of that commotion was done, Jon began to speak to Will. "You didn't see that killer come?" he asked.

"No," Will responded. "I just realized that your dog was acting strange and he wouldn't take his eyes off something. Soon I saw the killer running off."

"You had the dog with you. Why didn't you track him down?"

"I was too stunned by dad's death. I guess that didn't cross my mind."

"This guy has gone too far. If we catch him, he better get the worst penalty possible."

"Don't say *if* we catch him—we *are* going to catch him. His fun is going to stop very shortly."

The officers tried to continue with their job. They wanted that assassin captured as soon as possible.

CHAPTER 2

THE SILENT KILLER PROWLED THROUGH THE NIGHT. HE STOPPED IN FRONT OF A huge house. He walked over to the front doorstep and knocked. He waited awhile. He knocked again. That was when a young and bald man answered the door. "Can I help you?" he asked as he looked at the masked killer.

"No, but you can help yourself." the killer told him. He pulled out his knife from his coat and stabbed the man repeatedly to death. He had no time to waste.

The killer crouched down next to the dead man. He pulled out an envelope that had the man's name written on it—Mike Riley. He put it in his coat and left the house before anyone saw him there.

The killer silently roamed through the darkness. He paced himself over to where he dwelled in during the daytime. It was a cottage in the middle of some trees. It was somewhat old and the paint was starting to peel off.

The killer entered the small house and went into a small room. He grabbed a suitcase that had been there for years. There was a tag that had his address written on it hanging from the suitcase, but he did not care. He took his coat off and took the envelope with the man's name out. He placed the envelope in a slit that the suitcase had, but it was hanging out. He placed the coat inside the suitcase as well.

The killer changed into different clothing and put his mysterious and dark clothing in the suitcase. He wanted to be undisguised. When he was through, he grabbed the suitcase and left the cottage. He was going to leave the city so that no one would ever find him.

There was something else that the killer was carrying with him other than the suitcase—an explosive. He wanted a building to detonate when he left the city.

The mysterious man walked unmasked into the city. He knew that no one would recognize him. He just strolled right past many people, blending in with them. Then he stopped at a bus stop and waited patiently for a bus.

Minutes later, the bus arrived. The man entered it, paid the driver, and sat down. He wanted to go someplace very far from where everyone wanted him captured.

After forty-five minutes on the bus, the man got off. He saw a building in the distance. He walked over to it and entered it. He saw few people in it since it was began to close. He hurried and placed the bomb on top of a table filled with jewels. He began to run because the bomb was going to explode in thirty seconds.

As soon as the man was ten feet away from the exit, his foot went through a loose tile and it got stuck. He was not able to move. He tried to pull his foot out, but it was severely stuck. He kept on trying. He was not able to get it out. He needed to get it out or else he would also be caught in the huge explosion.

Miraculously the man freed his foot from the hole. He began to run toward the door. As soon as he opened it, the building instantaneously exploded.

The night was filled with the sound of rain falling from the dark sky. There was one thing that radiated the darkness. It was a small doctor's office in which only one doctor worked at. It was hidden deeply in the town. Very few people knew it even existed. To get back to the city, a person would have to walk for about three hours and a half.

In that office, the mysterious man was lying on a bed. He slowly opened his eyes. He noticed that he was in a strange place and he had bandages on his right arm and left leg. "What happened?" he asked. He looked over to his right and saw a man in a white coat with a receding hairline. "Where am I?"

"You're my first patient this month," the man answered. "I found you lying unconscious on the floor beside a building that had exploded. You are very lucky that you survived. Everyone else died. All you have are a couple of bruises and small burns. I picked you up and here you are."

The doctor walked over to the dark suitcase that the man had been carrying all along. "This was right beside your body when I found you," he explained. He took out the envelope that hung out of the suitcase. "Looks like perhaps your name is...Mike Riley?"

"It is?" asked the man.

The doctor looked at him strangely. "It's not?"

"You said it was."

"What's your name, sir?" the doctor asked as he raised an eyebrow.

"Mike...Riley."

"Where do you come from?"

"I don't know."

"Do you have any family or relatives that live around here?"

"I don't know."

"How old are you?"

"I don't know."

The doctor decided to ask one more question. "What is the last thing that you remember?"

"Waking up here."

"You don't remember anything else preceding that?"

The man sat up in his bed. "No. It's all blank."

The doctor figured out what was wrong with the man. "Looks like you're suffering from memory loss...Mr. Riley. You're going to live a totally different life now." He looked down at the tag that was on the black suitcase. "You're lucky that you have your address written down on here or else you wouldn't know where you lived." He studied it. "You live pretty far from here. It may take you a while to get there. Probably a relative of yours lives there and that person may be able to help you."

"When may I leave, doctor?"

"Tomorrow morning you'll be up and at it. You may leave then."

"Is my name actually Mike?"

"I don't know that, sir. Perhaps it is. Who knows where that envelope belongs? Perhaps someone gave it to you."

The man, now known as Mike, just nodded his head. He lied back down and said nothing further.

"You get some rest now, Mr. Riley. I'll probably see you in the morning. Have a good night."

Mike said nothing. He tried to go to sleep. He began to think what the next day would see him doing.

There were terrible images going through the mind of Mike Riley. He was seeing a sharp-bladed knife in motion and dark clothing swiftly moving. He heard yelling and many cries. He did not know what these images were and why they were there.

Mike abruptly sat up in bed. He took quick deep breaths. "It was only a dream," he assured himself. "Only a dream." He lied back down in bed. He wondered why he had such a cruel and violent dream. That was his first one and he would never forget it.

The morning arrived with its beautiful horizon. The sun rose up and greeted the land with another day. It made a nice reflection on a clear and blue lake. Swans waddled by and stepped into the lake. They gracefully floated on top of it.

A sweet breeze gently blew between the leaves of trees. A crow was crowing on one of the branches. It later flew off and landed in another tree. It began its crowing again from there. It was a nice morning.

Mike awoke from his sleep and looked around. He did not see the doctor. He slowly sat up in the bed and removed himself off of it. He heard the bird crowing off in the distance. It began to grow faint as if it were flying further and further away.

Soon the doctor came into Mike's sight. "Good morning," he said with a smile. "It's nice to see you up and about. Well, let's get going. We're going to have to get moving if you want to find out about your past life."

All Mike did was nod. He limped over to his suitcase, grabbed the handle, and pulled it off the table. "Let's go," he finally said.

The doctor got a hold of his keys. "I'll drive you to the city and then you're on your own from there. You'll just have to take the auto-bus. I'll give you some change for that in case you don't have any."

Mike stayed silent. He stood there and waited for the doctor to open the door. When he did, he slowly stepped outside.

The doctor locked the door and walked over to a white van. He opened the passenger door and then walked around to open the driver's door. When he and Mike were ready, they went on their way to the city.

On the way, Mike stared out the window and thought of what he would be doing when he arrived home. He knew he would not recognize anybody but they were going to be either friends or relatives. They would probably help him around and tell him what his actual name was. Yes, he had a feeling that someone would be there to help him and that the beginning of his confusing life would turn reasonable and understanding.

Thirty minutes had gone by and the men had arrived in the city. The doctor pulled over next to a sidewalk. "Well, Mike," he started. "It's been a pleasure meeting you. You're on your own now. I wasn't even supposed to leave the building, but I wanted to help you. Oh, and by the way, here." He reached into his wallet and handed Mike four quarters. "That's to pay the bus driver. It's not really going to be a dollar, but I just gave it to you in case you needed it."

Mike placed the quarters in his pocket. "Thanks," he said lowly. He opened the door and slowly stepped out of the van.

"Bye, Mr. Riley."

Mike said nothing. He closed the door and limped away from the van. He stopped at a bus stop that was nearby. He looked over and saw the doctor drive away. He wanted to know why he did not just take him to his house if he drove him all the way to the city.

A bus arrived ten minutes later. Mike leisurely stepped onto the bus. He paid the driver and got a seat. Moments later, after all the passengers were on, the bus drove off.

Mike did not know when was the time to get off. He looked at the tag with his address on it. He looked at the name of the city and then looked at the woman sitting beside him. He nudged her. "Hey," he said.

The woman, who was reading a book, looking at him through her reading glasses. "Yes?" she asked.

"Can you tell me when we get here?" He pointed to the name of the city.

The woman looked at it. "Are you a tourist, sir?"

"No," answered Mike. "It's just that...Yeah, I am a tourist I guess. So can you tell me when we get there?"

"Sure."

Mike just nodded with appreciation. He looked outside the window and viewed the city. The woman went back to reading her book.

Soon, when Mike was beginning to doze off, the woman tapped him on the shoulder and said, "Sir, we're here."

Mike opened his eyes. "Okay," he said tiredly. "Thanks for telling me."

"My pleasure." She looked down at his leg. "Do you need help?"

"No, thanks. I can handle it."

Mike stood up and limped down the aisle of the bus. He then stepped down from the bus. He began to walk down the sidewalk but he did not know where he was going. He knew that he needed to ask for directions to get to his house.

An hour had gone by and the last direction that Mike was told to go was down a rocky pathway. He walked down it and at last he found a cottage at the end of it, hidden by many trees. He was thinking why he would live in such a solitary place. It seemed so gloomy.

Mike finally reached the cottage. He knocked on the door and expected an answer. No one opened the door. He knocked again. When he saw that no one answered, he tried to twist the doorknob and the door opened. He was amazed to see that the door was left unlocked.

Mike stepped into the small house and closed the door behind him. "Hello?" he shouted. "Anyone home?" Silence. He looked around to see if there were any pictures, but he did not find any. "Did I live alone?"

There was a room down the hallway and Mike walked over to it and entered it. He saw that it was nearly empty. There was just a bed with no sheets and empty boxes on the floor. He looked into the closet and saw that there was nothing inside of it except for a few hangers. "Am I in the wrong house? It matched with the address."

Mike set his suitcase down on top of the bed. He unzipped it and the dark clothing was revealed. He pulled out the coat and looked at it for a moment. He put it on the bed and took out a hanger from the closet. He placed the coat on the hanger and hung it in the closet. The next thing he took out from the suitcase was the pair of pants. He hung those up as well.

After Mike was done, he said, "I'm going to need to fix this place up. It needs to be cleaned, dusted, repainted, and a whole bunch of other things." He sat on his bed. "I guess no one lived with me. I lived alone. I wonder if I left any phonebooks anywhere."

Mike stood up and walked out of the room. He looked inside a drawer that was in the living room. There were just a few cobwebs inside there. He closed the drawer and looked inside another one. There were papers inside. He took them out and unfolded them. They were blank so he placed them back inside.

Soon Mike stopped searching. "There's nothing to prove that I ever had a relative," he said quietly. "There aren't any pictures, letters, books, or anything like that. Why do I live by myself?"

Mike just sat on an old couch behind him. He thought about what he had to do. He knew that he had to renew the house. He had to buy new furniture and appliances. He did not know where he was going to get the money for it since he did not speak to anybody or live around anyone. His home was in the middle of nowhere, away from everything. Probably no one even visited or knew where he lived.

"How did I ever live like this?" Mike asked out loud as if he were speaking to someone else. "Why did I live like this?" He wished that he was able to get an answer to his questions, but he knew that he would not so he stopped questioning out loud. He actually expected an answer, but he did not know from where. Perhaps he will have another strange dream like he did the preceding night. Maybe he will have an answer in his dreams.

Mike stayed sitting on the couch. "I wonder how it was in my other life," he said nearly in a whisper. "I wonder what I did back then."

CHAPTER 3

NEARLY FIVE MONTHS HAD GONE BY VERY QUICKLY. THE CITY WAS AS BUSY AS IT always was. There was a difference though—it was not as hot as usual. The sun was behind a few clouds and the temperature was beginning to drop. It was about forty degrees out. Many people did not consider that as cold yet, but others did. Pretty soon, it would begin to snow.

The busy police station had a new chief. Everyone still wanted to find out who murdered the old one. It was still a mystery that they were not able to solve yet.

Jon and Will were in their office, filing papers when Susan came and told them some news. "Hey, we have a new guy."

"Who?" Jon asked as he tried to look out the doorway, but Susan was blocking his view.

"Come with me and I'll show you." She removed herself from the doorway.

Jon looked at his brother. "Are you coming?"

"I suppose," answered Will. He put a stack of papers down on a table.

Jon left the room and Will followed.

Susan walked to a man with black-brown hair and blue eyes. He was a little taller than she was and his weight was normal.

"This is Officer Mike Riley," she introduced.

"Hello," Jon greeted. He stuck his hand out for a handshake. "I'm Jon. It's a pleasure to meet you."

Mike shook his hand and said, "Hi." Then he looked over at Will and greeted him as well.

All Will said was, "Hi. I'm Will." He had a serious expression.

Later, around break time, Jon was speaking to Mike. He was inside his office. "So what do you think of the chief?" he asked.

"He's all right," answered Mike. "He can get a little crazy though."

"Yeah. He has a good sense of humor." He paused for a moment. "My father used to be the chief here around five months ago."

"What happened to him?"

"Some guy killed him. We never found out who he was. He was the serial killer at the time. He always hid his identity. We never had the chance to catch him. I don't think we will because he hasn't been heard of since those five months."

"Don't worry," Mike said. "We'll catch him. I'll make sure of that."

"I hope so. That guy escapes easily and I think he doesn't even live here anymore because there aren't anymore reports about him. He's still on our wanted list though."

"It doesn't matter where he is—we're still going to catch him. He can be in another country for all I care—I know he'll hit prison really soon."

"Sounds like you're very sure of yourself. That's a good trait to have."

Hours later it was time for the three men to go off duty. Susan was the only one that worked later. They bid their farewells to each other and then left the station.

Jon was speaking with Mike while they were walking outside. Will was standing by, but was not saying anything. He was getting the car key ready.

Mike told Jon something. "I live really far from here," he started. "I'm too tired to walk—my home is about forty-five minutes away. I don't want to take the city bus because it just drops me off half an hour away from my home, so it makes no difference. So, well, can you give me a ride home?"

"I would," Jon started, "but don't you have a police cruiser?"

Mike paused for a moment. "Well...I haven't gotten one yet. I know it sounds weird but that's how it is."

"Oh okay. Well, sure—we'll take you home." Jon looked at his brother. "Right?"

Will responded, "It's not like we have any time to lose."

"Okay, thanks," Mike said.

When they reached up to the cruiser, Will unlocked the back door and the passenger door. Then he walked around and unlocked the driver's door. He stepped inside the car and waited until the other two were inside. That was when he started the car up and drove off.

Mike gave Will directions to his house and it took twenty minutes to arrive there. The car stopped in front of the long pathway that led to the solitary house.

"Why do you live so far from everything?" Jon asked as he looked out his window and viewed the small house.

"I don't know," Mike answered. It was the only thing that he was able to say.

"Don't you get lonely over here? No one lives around this place."

"I've gotten used to it." He got off of the subject. "Well, thanks for the ride." He unlocked the door and opened it. "It was greatly appreciated."

"Don't mention it," Will said, nearly to himself.

When Mike stepped out of the car, he stuck his head inside and said, "Hey, Jon, do you think you could step out for a moment so that I can talk to you for a little bit?"

"All right," Jon replied as he unbuckled his seatbelt. He looked at Will. "Maybe you'll need to turn the engine off."

Will turned the key and the engine went off. He wanted to say something but he kept quiet.

Jon stepped out of the car. "I'll only be a minute." He closed the door.

Will sighed and leaned against the window.

"So what do you want to talk to me about?" Jon asked as he and Mike walked down the pathway.

Mike looked out to the trees. Then he faced Jon and questioned him. "Does your...?" He turned around and looked back at the car. He turned back around and continued his question. "Does your brother dislike me or something?"

"Why do you ask?"

They stopped walking because they had reached the front of the cottage. Mike answered Jon's question. "It's because he seems as if he does not want to talk to me. Did you see his expression when I first met him and when I asked for the ride home?"

Jon sighed. "I don't know," he answered. "Well he..."

"I really want to meet him but it doesn't look like he wants anything to do with me."

"He hasn't really acted like this toward anyone. He's changed ever since our father got murdered. He hasn't gotten over it yet. At least until we find the killer. It has nothing to do with you. Sooner or later, you'll be having a normal conversation with him."

Mike was quiet for a moment. He then broke his own silence. All he did was nod his head and say, "Okay. Thanks, Jon. I'll see you tomorrow."

"Goodbye, Mike."

Jon waved goodbye and walked down the pathway to the cruiser. He opened the door and stepped inside. He closed the door.

Will started up the car and backed up. He made a left turn and drove away from the lonely place.

Jon had to ask Will a question concerning what Mike told him. He looked straight through the windshield and asked, "So what do you think of Mike?"

Will answered, "I think he's all right. Why?"

"You didn't really speak to him so how can you have an opinion at all?"

"I'm just judging from what I *do* know."

"Okay. I was only curious. Are you going to speak to him more?"

"The station is for working, not conversing. If I had spare time, then I would get to know him better. The only way I'll get to know him is through the job."

Jon stayed silent. He did not want to say anything against what his brother was saying because he would never win.

Mike walked down the hallway and to his bedroom. He sat on his bed. He had bought that bed a week after he first arrived at the house. He also bought a couch. That was all he had because he was not able to afford any more furniture. When he had the money, he would probably get some more.

Mike also repainted the inside of the house. The paint used to be peeling off of the walls, but now it was smoothly painted pure white. The outside of the house would be repainted as soon as possible.

While Mike was removing his shoes, a thought crossed his mind. It was strange that he began his "new life" five months ago and during that time, the killer was not heard of. There was only one thing that he could think of, but he did not want to take it as true.

"No," Mike said to himself. "It can't be me. It's not me. I can't be the chief of police. I'm too young. The chief is dead and I'm going to find his assassin. I know that he's out there somewhere and he'll be captured soon. I feel it inside of me. Right now I'm feeling that he is very close."

The following day at the police station, Mike walked up to Jon and said, "I just got my cruiser."

"Really?" Jon asked. "That's great. When are you going to ride around in it?"

"I was thinking now but I wanted to know if you wanted to go with me."

"Sure. I was about to go in mine."

"But there's only one thing."

"What?"

"You're driving."

Jon was confused. "Why should I drive?" he asked. "It's your cruiser."

"Yeah, but you know your way around more than I do. I have to get used to it first."

Jon looked at him strangely and said, "Okay, but I still don't know why you don't at least try."

Jon and Mike left the police station and walked up to Mike's police car. Mike went into the passenger seat and Jon went into the driver's seat. Soon they were on the road.

While Jon was driving, he glanced over at Mike and asked, "You're not going to ask me to drive every time, right?"

"No, I'm not," Mike answered. "It's just for today. I'll get used to my way around and then I'll drive."

"Okay. That's good because…" He stopped for the reason that he noticed a driver speeding up ahead of him. He looked at the radar detector. "This guy's going eighty miles an hour. We have to stop him." He turned on the siren.

Sooner or later the driver pulled over because he knew that he was the one Jon was chasing.

"You step out," Jon told Mike. "It's your first time and you're going to have to do this a lot. Go on out there."

"All right," Mike said as he opened the door and stepped out of the car. He shut the door and walked over to the speeding black Chevrolet Blazer. He knocked on the window and signaled the driver to pull it down. The driver pulled it down.

Mike began to speak. "I caught you doing eighty miles an hour. That's past the speed limit, you know."

The driver looked at him from under his cap. "Eighteen miles ain't past the speed limit," he said.

"I said eighty," Mike corrected him. "License and registration please."

"What? Why you wanna see that for? I wasn't speeding. Just let me go on home. I ain't hurt nobody."

"Look, just do as I say and…" Mike looked over to the right side of the driver. He saw an empty beer bottle there. "How many of those did you have?"

"What?" the driver asked as he looked down at his right side. He picked up the beer bottle. "This? I just had like about two of these."

"We'll see about that. Step out of the vehicle please."

"What? Now you want me to step out of my car? No way."

"I'm not going to say it again. Step out of the vehicle, sir."

"No 'cause you can't make up your mind. First you tell me to take out my license and now you want me to step out of the car. Which one of them do you want me to do? I ain't steppin' out."

Jon had been hearing all of the commotion. He stepped out of the car, shut the door, and walked over to where Mike was. "Do as he says and step out of the vehicle," he ordered the driver.

"Hey, where'd you come from?"

"After you step out, we'll let you go, okay?"

"Really?" the driver asked with delight. He looked at Mike. "Why ain't you say that to me before? I would have stepped out." He opened the door and when he began to step out, he slipped.

Jon caught his arm and stood him on his feet. He looked over at Mike. "You do the testing," he told him.

"Okay," said Mike. He looked at the driver. "Recite the alphabet."

"What am I—in kindergarten? Why are you askin' me to say the alphabet for?"

"Just do as I tell you and stop making things so complicated."

The driver sighed and started to recite the alphabet. He did well so far until he confused *m* and *n*. Then he switched *p* and *t*. After that he restarted. He was not able to pass *t*.

"Okay," Mike said after the driver was done. "Now put your right foot in front of your left one, spread your arms, and walk by putting one foot in front of the other."

"That's so easy," the driver commented. He began to walk like how Mike told him to but he was not able to last. He tripped immediately and Mike caught him by the arm and stood him up.

"That's it," Jon said. "You're going to good ol' jail."

"What?" the driver shouted. "I thought you said that you'll let me go after you were done."

"You know what I meant—let you go to jail." He took out a pair of handcuffs and arrested the man.

"No," the driver said. "This ain't right. I'm gonna call the cops. This ain't right."

"Let's go," Jon told him as he began walking him to the police car. He opened the backdoor and told the man to go inside the car. As soon as he was done he went over to Mike. "Call a towing company and tell them to tow this guy's car."

"All right," Mike agreed.

Hours had passed after Mike and Jon took the drunk driver to jail. It was now time for Mike to leave the police station. Jon and Susan were going home as well. Will was going to work late.

As the three officers exited the police station, Jon said, "Nice job today, Mike."

"Oh, thanks," Mike replied.

"You did all right for your first try."

Mike changed the subject. "Let me ask you a favor."

"Okay."

"I need to fix my house up a bit. The outside needs to be repainted and the inside needs to be a little organized and dusted. I haven't had time to do it and I don't think I can do it alone. Can you come over someday and help me?"

"Sure," Jon responded. "That was the way I made money in the past. I used to paint people's doors and polish a lot of wood."

Mike looked at Susan. "Do you want to help?"

"I'd be glad to, Mike," answered Susan. "When do you want us to come over?"

"I guess Thursday's a good day, right?"

"Yeah, I think so, too."

Jon also agreed.

Mike took out a piece of paper and a pen to write his address down. He gave a copy to both Jon and Susan.

"Okay," said Susan. "I'll be there. Bye, Mike." She gave him a hug and then faced Jon. "Bye, Jon." She gave him a hug and after that she began to walk toward her police car.

Jon and Mike said goodbye to Susan. After she left, Jon said, "Well, I have to go to the bus stop since Will's taking the cruiser home tonight. I'll see tomorrow, all right, Mike?"

"All right," Mike responded. "So long, Jon."

"Goodbye." Jon then turned around and crossed the street and began to walk along the sidewalk.

Mike sighed. He looked at his police car. "Let's see if I can try to drive this thing home."

Mike opened the driver's door and stepped inside the car. He closed the door and sat there to think things over for a moment. After he was done, he put the key in the ignition and started the car up. He watched previously at how Jon backed up the car, so he tried to do the same thing. He moved the rod and began to back the car up.

Soon Mike was facing the road. He wanted to see if he was able to get there. He started to move the car forward. He stopped and began to move the car again. Now he decided to keep on moving the car. He started to swirl around a little bit so he stopped. "I can't do this," he said as he slammed his fist on the steering wheel. "I'm probably going to get into an accident. They're going to think that I'm driving drunk. I'm going to take the bus."

Mike started to think for a moment. "There has to be a way I could learn how to drive." Strangely he already had a driver's license because of the identity he took. It was a long story on what happened.

Mike thought about the driving situation for a moment. He did not want to ask Jon to teach him because it would be downright embarrassing. He did not want to take classes because he would not have time for them. He had to practice somehow, but he had to take his car to his house in order to practice. How was he going to learn how to drive?

"I have to learn one way or another," Mike told himself. Suddenly something came to him. "There's only one way to do it."

Mike arrived at an arcade. He left the police station by taking the city bus and he went home. He dressed out of his police uniform and put on casual clothing. When he was ready, he left his house and walked to the nearest arcade, which was nearly forty-five minutes away.

When Mike entered through the doors of the arcade, he saw neon lights everywhere and he heard loud rock music playing. He paid two dollars to enter and then he looked around. He was looking for a special game to play.

Before he decided on which game to play, Mike went over to a token machine to get a few tokens. He placed in a twenty-dollar bill and he received forty tokens. He put them in his right pocket. He thought that he was going to use them all.

After Mike was done with that, he went back to searching for a game to play. He began to walk around. He saw a few action and fighting games.

There was a pinball machine up ahead of him. Then that was when the special game appeared. It was a racing game in which the driver got inside a car and watched the road on the screen as he or she drove. The driver actually moved the steering wheel and the rod and the car really moved. It felt as if the driver was really driving.

Mike walked over to that and entered the car. He had to put in two tokens, so he did. The screen said to press the start button so he did. Now there was a voice counting down from three. As soon as it said to go, Mike pressed down on the right pedal. He was driving through the city. He saw at least two cars ahead of him. He swerved over to the left so that he would not hit one. He kept on driving. He looked down at the speedometer and saw that he was going forty miles an hour.

Soon Mike saw that he had to make a right turn so he did. He hit the side of the road. He moved away from the side and continued to drive. He saw that there was a stoplight up ahead. He had to calculate when to stop. He pressed on the left pedal and began to slow down as soon as he thought it was a good time to do it. The car stopped at least twenty feet away from the light.

Mike moved forward a little bit and stopped. Soon the light turned green and he continued to drive. He went on the side of the road again because he had to move out of the way of cars ahead of him.

"I have to stay off the side of the road," Mike told himself. He moved the car more to the left and he was back on track.

Mike continued to drive and he saw that he was going sixty-five miles an hour now. He knew that he had to slow down so he took some pressure off of the pedal. That made him go twenty miles an hour. He had to get it just right.

Suddenly there was the sound of a police car. The word *speeding* then appeared on the screen in big red letters. Mike had to restart. "Aw…man," he said. He looked to his right and saw a young guy standing next to the car and watching him play. The guy looked like he was about fifteen or sixteen years old. He had on a cap placed on backward, black hair, a red basketball jersey shirt, and he looked Spanish.

"You've played this before?" Mike asked.

"Yeah, it's awesome," the guy commented.

"How many times did you have to restart in order to get it right?"

"I would have to say like fifty times. It's pretty hard. It's like real life driving."

"Yeah, I can see that. Do you drive yet?"

"I have my permit."

"Does this game help you in some way?"

"Actually it does. I just remember all the mistakes that I made in the game and I try not to do them in actual driving. This game helps out a lot."

Mike decided not to say anything further. He was glad that the young teen did not ask him why he kept questioning him about the game and driving. He just faced the screen and inserted two more tokens. He played another game.

Later Mike ran out of tokens because he had restarted so many times. He looked to see if the guy was still there and he was. "I'm getting more tokens, all right? You can play the game if you want."

The teen just said, "No, it's okay. I'll watch the car for you so that no one would go in. No. As a matter of fact, I'll go inside and act as if I'm going to play so that no one would be able to come in. Even if I see people coming towards this car, I'll tell them that I'm already playing."

Mike was shocked at how persistent that teenager was being. All he said was, "Okay, thanks." Then he began to walk toward the token machine. He put in another twenty-dollar bill and received forty tokens.

"I'm wasting my money on a game," Mike informed himself. He sighed and walked back to the car.

The teen got out of the car as soon as he saw Mike coming. Mike entered the car and prepared himself for another game.

The teenager said, "Let's see if you can beat it now."

It was a good thing that the arcade stayed open until six o'clock in the morning because Mike stayed playing the racing game until one in the morning. The teenager had left two hours ago and he had wished Mike good luck.

The other good thing was that Mike actually got the hang of the game. He made less and less mistakes. He stopped going on the side of the road and his calculating was much better. The police officer never pulled him over again. He thought he was ready to really drive. He was prepared to capture that wanted murderer if he ever saw him on the streets. Obviously he would probably never get his chance to see him on the streets.

CHAPTER 4

JON WAS SLEEPING FROM A LONG DAY'S OF WORK. HE WENT TO SLEEP EARLY SO that he would be able to wake up early for the next day of work. Nearly every single day was filled with working.

There were strange noises outside. They were not so loud so they did not awaken Jon. He was actually a deep sleeper compared to his brother. Will would wake up if someone stepped a foot inside his room. The thing was that he slept with his door wide open.

Suddenly the noises became louder. Jon tried to ignore it by putting his pillow over his head. He kept on hearing the strange noises so he sat up in his bed and whispered, "What's that?" Something came to him. "Could that be *him*?"

Jon got out of his bed and walked down the hallway. He walked to the front door and looked out his window. He saw a group of teenagers throwing rocks at the fence and the window. He sighed and opened the door. He looked over at the teenagers and shouted, "What are you guys doing out so late? Don't you know that it's past your curfew?"

The person that seemed to look like the leader of the group turned around and faced Jon. He had a black jacket on and blue baggy sweatpants. There were three other males and one female. Although it was cold, she was dressed with a pair of really short jean shorts and a tank top that covered half her chest.

The leader said, "We don't care if it's past our curfew. We go out anyway."

"It's illegal for you guys to do this. You guys are going to get caught and…"

"We don't care," the female responded. "We know you're a cop. We don't care 'cause we know that you can't do anything about it."

"Oh really?" Jon asked.

"Yeah," the leader responded. "We're going to hang out as long as we want to and you cops ain't gonna stop us."

"My brother should be coming soon from his job."

"Let him come," the female told him. "He's not going to tell us what to do, either. What makes him any better than you?"

"Why don't you guys stay here and wait until he comes? You guys think that no one can control you, right? Hang out here for a while and have fun destroying my fence."

"We'll stay," said the female. "We'll wait 'til the other cop comes."

The group began to laugh. "Cops think that they can tell us what to do just because they're cops," a member said. The rest began to laugh again.

Jon sighed. "I hate dealing with teens," he whispered. "They think they're so bad."

The teenagers began to throw rocks at other people's doors. "Let's wake these people up," the leader said.

"No, guys," Jon shouted. "Don't do that."

The female turned around and said, "You can't tell us what to do. Why don't you come over here and stop us? Right now, you're just a regular guy. And even if you were on duty, we still wouldn't listen to you."

Jon sighed again. The female was right. He was not able to do anything at that moment since he was not on duty. All he could do was keep them there for awhile.

Soon Jon saw a car pulling in. It was a police car. Will had just arrived home. He shut off the headlights and stepped out of the car.

The leader turned around and said, "Hey look, he's finally here." The rest of the group turned around and stood there.

"What's going on?" Will asked as he began to walk toward Jon. "Why are you out here so late?"

Jon answered, "Look over there and you'll find out." He pointed towards the teenagers. "They woke me up because they were throwing things on the fence and the window. They're trying to wake up everyone in the neighborhood."

Will glanced over at them.

"I told them that you were coming and they said that they didn't care and that you weren't going to be able to tell them what to do."

Will started off by asking the teenagers a question. "Why are all of you out here so late? Didn't you know that your time out here is up?"

"Yeah," the leader answered. "I don't know why we need a time limit for. It's so stupid."

"Well, if you made up the laws, they would be even more stupid."

The group looked at the leader.

"I won't question you people anymore." He unlocked the back-door of the car and stood behind the opened door. "You're coming with me. Get in the car."

"Hey," the female started. "Don't tell us to go in the car. You can't tell us what to do, cop."

"And you can't tell *me* what to do. Now get in the car."

The four males were about to walk over, but they stopped when the female said, "We're not going to go inside the car. You're going to have to come over and make us."

"Do you really want me to come over there and make you? I don't think you want me to do that."

Will handcuffed the four males and then he looked at the female. "It's your turn. Let's go."

"No," she said. "You're not going to handcuff me."

"Don't make me walk over there. Get over here and shut your mouth."

The female began to shift her body a little to the right. Will already knew what she was trying to do. "Don't even try to run off because I will catch you and put you through your worst misery. If you think I'm kidding, why don't you try and do it?"

Those words made the girl not even think about running. She walked over to Will and he handcuffed her. "Now get in the car," he told all of them. He stayed behind the opened door.

The leader looked inside the car and said, "We can't all fit back here."

"Isn't that too bad?" Will asked. "Get in there and make yourselves fit. Sit on each other's laps if you have to. I don't care. Just get in the car."

The leader looked inside again. Then he went inside the car. The other males entered in after him. They had to really squeeze themselves to fit in the backseat. The female came in and she had to sit on one of the males' laps.

After that was over, Will closed the door. He looked at Jon and said, "I'll be back."

Jon stood there and watched as his brother entered the car and drove off.

While Will was driving down the road, he began to speak to the leader. "Hey, wise guy, lead me to your house."

"Are you talking to me?" the leader asked.

"Yes, I'm talking to you. Lead me to your house and if you lie to me, I'll find out where you really live and you'll be in double the trouble you're in right now."

"We're going to my house? Why?"

"Don't worry about it. Just tell me where it is."

The leader led Will to where he lived. Will parked the car in the driveway and then he stepped out of the car. He opened the back-door and said to the leader, "Get out of the car."

The leader stepped out of the car and said, "The guy that was sitting next to me is my brother."

"Then he has to step out as well."

The brother stepped out. Will took the handcuffs off of both of them and then walked up the walkway with them. He saw that there was still light in the house. He rang the doorbell.

"Why you doin' this to us?" the brother asked.

"Stay silent," Will told him.

Soon the door opened. A woman answered it. "Yes?" she asked. She looked at the two teenagers. "Oh my. What happened, officer?"

"These two were out in the street throwing rocks at people's doors. First of all, they're not supposed to be doing that. Secondly, it's way past their curfew. They are not supposed to be out this late."

"I didn't know that they left the house. They probably sneaked out."

"Well, I advise to keep everything locked and to make sure that you know if they leave the house or not because if I ever catch either one of them in the streets late at night again, they will be arrested...and you will be, too."

The mother was shocked. She told her sons to enter the house. She was very angry with them. "Thank you, officer," she said.

Will turned around and said, "Good night, ma'am." As he walked down the walkway, he heard the woman yelling at the boys. He sighed and entered his car. It was now time to take the rest of the teenagers home.

The last one that Will had to take home was the female. While he was driving to her house, she said, "I don't even know why I'm listening to what you're saying. I don't even listen to my parents, so why should you be any different?"

Will answered, "Do I look like your parent?"

"Do you even have kids?"

"No and if I did, they would not even come close to being like you."

The female stayed quiet. Now she was trying to think of something.

When the thought came to her, she began to cry.

Will said, "Don't even try it. Don't try to act as if you're crying so that I won't take you home."

"I'm not acting," the female snapped. "I'm really crying."

"I wouldn't care anyway. I don't have sympathy for anyone."

"I bet the other cop would."

"I'm not him, am I? I've been through a lot of people who tried to get out of these situations. They try to act funny, they cry, they try to make me feel sorry for them, they compliment me, and they even try to tell me sad events that have happened in their lives. I don't care. It's not going to stop me from arresting them."

Will parked next to the driveway of the home that the female lived in. He turned off the engine of the car and stepped out. He walked over to the backdoor and opened it. He pulled the female out of the car and took the handcuffs off of her hands.

While they were walking to the front door, the female said, "I'm cold. Can you do something about that?"

"No, I can't," Will answered. "If you wore clothes, then you wouldn't be cold."

The girl stayed quiet. She walked up to the door with Will. Before Will knocked on the door, the girl stepped in front of him and said, "Please don't. Don't tell my mother. She'd kill me."

"I thought your parents couldn't tell you what to do. Why should you be afraid of them?"

"Just don't do it."

The girl buried her head in Will's chest and began to cry hysterically. Will grabbed her arm and placed her beside him. Then he knocked on the door. He looked through the window and saw that it was very dark inside.

"It looks like everyone is asleep," said Will.

"Then take me next door," the girl said desperately as she wiped away her tears. "The neighbors are awake."

Will ignored her and knocked on the door again. Now he heard someone shout, "Who is it?"

"Police," Will answered. "Open the door."

The woman opened the door. She was in her nightgown. "What is it? Why do you have my daughter?"

"I'm sorry if I woke you up, ma'am," Will started off. He explained everything to the woman.

After Will was done explaining, the woman angrily pulled her daughter inside the house and slapped her. She began yelling at her in Spanish.

Will walked away and said, "Have a good night, ma'am."

Later Will arrived at his house. He stepped out of the car, closed the door and locked it. He walked up to the front door of the house and opened it. He saw Jon sitting on the couch waiting for him.

"Why are you still up?" Will questioned. "It's late."

"I wanted to know what happened," Jon replied.

"I just sent them to their houses."

"Did they listen to you?"

"Of course they listened to me."

Will began to walk down the hallway. "I'm going to bed. Good night."

Jon decided to get some rest as well. After all, tomorrow was another day to wake up early.

The following day was not such a big day for Jon or Susan. They worked their normal hours. Mike and Will had to stay and work late. It was going to be a long day for them.

Jon and Susan left the station after hours of working. The other two continued to do their job. They were going to spend more hours of working.

It was nearing midnight. Will and Mike were able to leave the station now. They did not even speak to each other the entire time they were working.

While the two officers were walking out of the police station, Will said, "So do you like the job so far?"

Mike could not believe that Will was actually speaking to him. He answered, "Yeah, it's all right."

"Have you always thought of having this job?"

"No."

"Have you made any arrests yet?"

"Yeah, I have. I arrested this drunk guy."

"You're going to have much more of them. There's always an idiot driving drunk in the streets at night. Sometimes in the day as well. Was it hard?"

"It was hard to get him out of the car."

"You'll learn to be tough on people. Last night I arrested five teens for being out on the streets late at night."

"Teens?" Mike asked sharply.

"Yep. They're one of the hardest people to control for some officers. They listened to every word I said. At first, they were answering back with their smart mouths. Then I got their attention."

"Wow," Mike commented as he thought about that. After he was done thinking of that, he thought of questioning Will about something. "Don't you ever think about getting killed on the job?"

"That's the last thing that crosses my mind," answered Will. "I'm always prepared for everything."

"Has anyone ever pulled a gun out on you?"

"Actually someone has. It was a killer that had invaded a home and killed two people. I arrived on the scene when he was in another home. I entered the house with three other officers. The killer was inside a girl's room. I confronted him and he pointed his gun at me. He told me to back away or else he'd shoot. I drew my gun at him and I told him that I would shoot him before he was even able to pull the trigger. He put the gun to the girl's head and said he'd shoot her if I didn't put my gun down."

"So what'd you do?"

"I snickered lowly and started to lower my gun. I acted as if I was about to put down, but in a quick flash, I raised my gun and shot the killer in the shoulder. The killer dropped to the ground. And eventually we arrested him. He's spending life in prison."

"That's good."

Suddenly Will got off the subject. "Well, it's been nice meeting you," he said.

"Yeah. It's been nice meeting you, too. See you tomorrow."

"So long." Will walked over to the police car. He unlocked the driver's door and stepped inside. He shut the door, started the car, and soon drove off.

Mike looked over at his police car. He did not know if he was ready to drive it yet. "At night?" he whispered to himself. "No way." He did not want to drive in the darkness. He was planning on trying it the next day. For now, he was going to take the city bus again.

The next morning at the police station there was some news. A team of officers was called to go to a house in which four people invaded. Of course Mike and the rest of the officers went. They had to rush over to the house so Mike went in the same police car as Susan. He knew that he would not be able to make it if he drove his own car.

When the officers arrived at the house, they stepped out of their cars. Will, Susan, and three other officers went into the house. They had their guns in handy in case of anything.

Susan began to walk up the stairs. She had her gun close to her chest and pointed upward. She walked up the stairs slowly. When she reached the top, she saw a man with a mask covering half his face inside a room.

Susan pointed her gun at him and yelled, "Don't move!"

The man put his hands up in the air. Then he slowly turned around. He still had a gun in his hand though.

"Put the weapon on the floor," Susan ordered him.

The man hesitated.

"Now!"

The man put the gun on the floor. He stood back up and put his hands back in the air.

Susan walked over to him and frisked him. She saw that he had no weapons on him so she arrested him. She walked with him outside the house and placed him inside her police car.

Soon two other criminals were caught. There was one more left.

Mike saw a young woman starting to run. She was not that far away from him. "Hold it right there!" he shouted at her.

The woman stopped and turned around. "I was running from those guys that went inside my house," she said.

"Really?" Mike asked. "They're all already caught."

"They are? I thought they were still inside."

"Why don't you stay here? Let me ask you some questions concerning the invaders."

"No, that's all right."

"I need to question everyone in the home."

The woman was silent. She was stumbling over what she was going to say.

"I am going to arrest you, young lady."

"Why?" the woman snapped. "I had nothing to do with those guys. Yeah, I hung out with them. But I wasn't doing anything. They were doing all the actions."

"It doesn't matter. You're still going to be arrested."

The woman looked down at the floor. She saw someone step right next to Mike. She looked up and saw Will. She looked down at his shoes again and back up at him.

"What's going on here?" Will asked.

"He's arresting me for no reason," answered the woman.

"She's the other criminal that you guys were looking for."

"Come on," Will told her. "Put your hands behind your back. And please don't make me repeat it."

"But why are you arresting me if I didn't do anything? Those guys were doing all the actions. I was just hanging with them. I told them to stop it because it wasn't nice."

"We're arresting you because you were with them."

"But I wasn't participating in any of their actions."

"It doesn't matter. You were in there with them. If a bomb exploded inside that building, you would be killed as well because you were hanging with the other guys. You didn't do anything but you still got killed. Now put your hands behind your back."

The woman remained silent. She did as Will told her.

Will arrested her and walked with her to the police car. He opened the door and placed her in there. He then shut the door.

Mike was amazed at how Will was able to handle people so easily. He thought that possibly he would be able to do that as well.

It was a day off for the officers at last. Although it was a day of relaxation, they still did a little bit of work. It had nothing to do with their job though.

Mike was at his house waiting for Susan and Jon to arrive. They were going to help him with his house. It seriously needed some work done on it.

Susan arrived first, but Jon came only minutes after. Mike greeted them outside.

"You live *here*?" Susan asked as she looked around.

"Yep," Mike answered.

"Why do you live in such a silent and lonely place?"

"The thing is—I don't know why. I'm planning on moving anyway."

Jon questioned, "Then why do you want your house fixed up?"

"Because I'm getting it ready for the next hermit that wants to live here."

About fifteen minutes later, the three of them got to work. Susan stayed inside and dusted many things off. She swept the floors and organized everything. The two men began to repaint the house and make it look less obsolete.

Mike grabbed a ladder and climbed on the roof. He prepared himself to paint the rooftop brick red, the color it was before. He had to chip many things away before he began painting. The paint looked so old, but he was going to take care of that.

Hours later, after Mike had just finished, Jon shouted from below, "Hey, Mike, what do you think?"

"I'll be right there," Mike shouted back. He climbed down the ladder and walked in front of the cottage. He took a good look at it. It looked much better.

Mike nodded his head in approval. "Looks good," he said.

"Yes, it does," agreed Jon.

"Let's see how it looks inside now."

The two of them entered the cottage and immediately noticed that it was well organized. The cobwebs were gone and there was not anymore dust on the cabinets and drawers.

"Looks like she did good," commented Mike.

Susan then appeared. "So how do you like it?" she asked.

"It's great," Mike replied. "You did a good job. This place is now nice and neat."

"So how much are we getting for all of this, Mike?" Jon asked.

Mike put on a confused look. "What?"

Jon laughed. "I'm just joking. It was actually kind of fun doing this." He looked at the front door and said, "Well, I'll see you two tomorrow."

"You're leaving already?" asked Mike.

"Yeah. Will and I have to go to some meeting."

"Okay. Bye, Jon."

Jon said goodbye to Susan and Mike and they bid their farewells to him. Then he went out the door and left.

Susan took a deep breath and let it out. She faced Mike and asked, "So what do you do here?"

Mike answered, "When I get too bored of doing nothing, I stand outside and watch everything going on around me. I feel the wind blowing and the sun's heat. I see foxes chasing a rabbits and a badgers trying to make homes."

"Have you ever been on the other side of the trees?"

"Oh yeah—plenty of times. It's really nice over there. Do you want to go see it?"

"Sure."

Mike and Susan left the cottage. They began to walk behind it and through the trees. There were many strange noises in the small forest.

"There used to be many birds here," Mike started. "But I guess they're leaving because of the cold weather. They say it's going to snow soon."

"Are you a hunter?" Susan questioned.

"No. I don't like killing animals. I think they should enjoy their lives while they're here just like we do. Yeah, we need to eat but why eat the same species all the time? Why not eat a snake? How come we can't eat a giant lizard or an elephant? Do you understand what I'm saying?"

Susan nodded. "I see you care a lot."

Mike did not reply to that. All he said was, "We're almost there."

Soon they were there. The view was amazing. There was a beautiful and tranquil lake in the middle of all the grass and the trees. The sun was reflecting off of the blue and clear water. There were also magnificent mountains in the backgrounds. They were behind a white mist.

Susan was very astounded. "Oh Mike," she said as she looked around. "This is incredible."

Mike nodded. "This is the place that I go to when I'm having a bad day. It makes me feel more relaxed and calm."

"I wonder how it'll look when it snows."

Mike faced over to the lake and said, "I look forward to seeing it."

Three days had gone by. Snow continuously fell from the sky. It began to leave a white and crystal blanket on the streets. The temperature was two degrees Fahrenheit and many people were walking down the streets with thick coats and jackets on. It was a very cold day.

There was a woman coming out of a supermarket with her teenage daughter. The daughter was disrespecting her mother a lot. She was hitting her and telling her to shut her mouth. The mother was not able to take it anymore.

"How can you do this to me in the middle of the streets?" the mother asked.

"So?" replied the daughter. "I'm not the one being embarrassed."

"If you keep up with your violence, I'm going to go tell those police officers over there."

"Go ahead and tell 'em. I don't care. It's not like they're going to do anything. I've punched one in the nose for trying to arrest me for stealing. I've kicked another one for trying to stop me from smoking. So why don't you go ahead and tell 'em? I'm not afraid."

The mother was now in tears. She was too desperate. She saw two officers, Jon and Susan. She walked up to them and began to plead. "Please, officers," she started. "Talk with my daughter. She is insane. She hits me, she curses at me, and she does horrible things. She's unstoppable. She is too violent."

"Where is she?" Jon asked.

The woman turned around and pointed. "Right there," she answered as she wiped away a tear with her shirt.

The girl was the one that walked over. "Hey what's up?" she said.

"Why are you so disrespectful to your mother?" questioned Jon.

"Because she pisses me off. She shouldn't get in the way when she pisses me off."

"So violence is the only way to show it?"

"Yeah. I'm violent toward anyone and you're not going to stop me."

Jon began to speak to her but the girl kept smiling and saying, "Yeah, yeah, yeah, yeah." She said that repeatedly.

Jon went up to her and before he was able to say anything, the girl pushed him away. "Get away from me. Nothing you do or say is going to stop me. I've committed seven crimes in under six hours." She began to laugh.

"Don't ever push an adult like that," Susan told the girl. "I don't care how big and bad you think you are. You're never going to do that again. You understand me?"

The girl began to laugh.

Jon went to go speak to the devastated mother. He was trying to calm her down and tell her that everything was going to be all right.

"What is so funny?" question Susan. "I'm not saying anything that's funny."

The girl replied, "It may not be funny to you. We all have different tastes."

Susan kept on speaking to the girl. The girl started to laugh. She asked, "Do you think I'm listening to you?"

"You better be," Susan told her.

The girl laughed again. "Well, I'm not. You can't do anything about it, either."

"Neither can you."

The girl lifted up her hand. "Don't make me hit you. I've hit every member of my family before, even my grandmother. You're not any different."

At that moment, Will and Mike arrived. "What's the problem now?" questioned Will.

Susan explained everything to him.

Mike looked at the girl and said, "You need to show some more respect." He started to say something but the girl kept repeating the word *ignoring* over and over again.

Before Will said anything, Mike grabbed the girl's arm and said, "You won't be ignoring me."

The girl released herself from Mike's grip. "Don't touch me," she said. "I've hit a cop in the face before for doing what you just did, so I advise you not to do that."

"I advise you to keep your mouth shut because you're nothing but a teenage punk."

"Don't call me that."

"I can call you whatever I want. Don't tell me what to do."

"Whatcha gonna do about it?"

"What are *you* going to do about it—that's the question."

Mike grabbed the girl's arm and began walking with her. "You and I are going to take a ride for a while." He faced the mother. "We'll be right back."

The girl began to speak, but Mike interrupted her. "From what I know about you, if someone hit you in the face or spoke to you like you spoke to us, you would beat the living hell out of them."

"Damn right I would."

Mike opened the backdoor of his car and placed the girl inside. He walked around his car and took a deep breath and let it out. He was prepared to drive again. He drove earlier on his way to and from work.

Mike entered the car and started it up. He began to drive. While he was, he started to speak to the girl. "Why do you enjoy hitting your mother?"

"She keeps pissing me off. This is the way I see it—if she knows I'm going to hit her, then why does she get in my way? It's like you can't teach an old dog new tricks. If he does something wrong, then you hit him. If he knows you're gonna hit him, then he won't do it no more."

"First of all, your mother is not an animal. You don't have the right to hit her. If you mess around with someone and they hit you, you would hit that person back, right?"

"Yeah. I'd beat them up."

"That's exactly what your mother needs to do to you, but she's afraid of you. Believe me, if you were my daughter, I'd beat the living hell out of you until you learn."

The girl was finally quiet.

"Put it this way—picture yourself in your mother's shoes. If your children hit you, you would hit them back because that's the way you are. You think it isn't right. Well, it isn't right to hit your mother. Got that?"

The girl remained silent.

"Look, you wouldn't want to live without a mother. Take it from me. You wouldn't want to live without a family. I've lived without a family for as long as I can remember. Believe me—it's hard. No one's there for you when you need help. No one's there to congratulate you when you've done something right. No one's there for anything that you do. You're alone. I'm alone. So, enjoy your mother now because tomorrow you may not have her there for you anymore."

About half an hour later, Mike came back with the girl. The mother was still crying. She was hoping that something went through her daughter's head.

The girl walked up to her mother and hugged her. "I love you," she said.

The woman cried even more. "I love you, too," she responded as she hugged her daughter really tight.

Jon looked at Mike and said, "Good job."

Will also said something. "It looks like you've got it. Nice work."

"Thanks," Mike replied.

The woman walked up to Mike and hugged him also. "Thank you," she told him. "Thank you for helping my daughter."

"You're welcome," said Mike.

It was very busy back at the police station. There were many people walking back and forth. The day was just beginning.

Suddenly everyone heard a voice shout, "Good morning, everybody!" It was the chief of police. He was always in a good mood. He was probably in a better mood because he never shouted like that. "I hope everyone has a nice and cold day today." He then went into his office.

Susan was putting some papers away when a woman with short brown hair walked up to her and asked, "Excuse me, ma'am, but where can I find Will…?"

"He's over there," Susan responded before the woman can even finish saying the full name.

The woman looked over to where Susan was pointing. There were about four men. "Which one is he?"

"Oh he's the tall, handsome one with the dark hair."

The woman smiled. "Thank you." She walked away.

The woman walked over to Will. She stopped in front of him and said, "Excuse me. Will?"

Will faced her. "Yes, that's me."

First the woman told Will who she was. She worked for a police department in Illinois.

"What is this about?" questioned Will.

"I came here to talk about your father."

"What's the matter with him?"

"We know that he had been killed about five months ago. He was killed by a deadly assassin that was never able to be caught."

"Okay, but what do you need to tell me?"

"What I need to tell is that we know who the murderer of the chief of police is."

CHAPTER 5

WILL WAS NOT ABLE TO GIVE CREED TO WHAT HE JUST HEARD. THE ONLY THING he was able to say was, "What?"

"It may be hard to believe after all of these months but we know who the killer is," the woman explained.

"Who is it?"

"It's this young man that we caught. He was arrested for killing a young girl."

"How do you know he killed my father?"

"He admitted to it. He told us that he used to do his murders over here and that he killed the chief of police."

"Did he wear those dark clothes?"

"Yes, he did. I personally think that it's him."

Will was so shocked, he was not able to say anything.

"Do you want to come with us for a couple of days and speak to the man?"

Will faced the woman and answered, "Yes, I do. I want to make sure that this guy is tortured. He completely deserves it."

"We'll take you with us tomorrow morning. It's been nice talking to you. Goodbye." The woman left.

Will went over to speak to Jon who was conversing with Mike. "I need to speak to you," he said.

"What is it?" Jon asked.

"They found out who killed dad."

Jon abruptly stood up. "Are you serious? Who is it?"

"Some killer that was caught in Illinois. I'm going there tomorrow."

"Wait a minute—who told you this?"

"Some lady who works on these cases."

"How do you know that it's the real killer?"

"She seemed pretty sure. I don't think that they'll catch the wrong guy."

"What if they did? This guy was so hard to catch when he was here. How was he caught there? I mean, it's pretty strange."

"They probably trapped him or tricked him into going somewhere. Look, the lady even said that he wore those clothes of his."

Jon shook his head. "I don't know. I find it strange that he would suddenly show up after all these months. As stubborn as you are, I don't know how you can believe some stranger."

"She works on cases like this."

"So do I."

It was silent for a moment.

Will broke the silence by saying, "I'm going there tomorrow in the morning."

"You're going to see the supposed killer?"

"Yep. I'll be there only for a few days."

Jon did not say anything.

Then Will asked, "Are you coming?"

"No," answered Jon. "I'll stay here."

"Why? Is that how much you care about your own father? You don't even want to come and see who killed him?"

"I do care but I'm not going. I have a feeling that they caught the wrong guy."

"It's up to you." Will turned around and walked away.

Susan had been standing there for the past fifteen seconds. She asked, "Where is he going?"

"He's going to Illinois to talk to the supposed killer of our father."

"They found him?"

"I don't know. I really don't think so."

Mike was looking at the beautiful scene behind his house after a long day. He saw the snow covering the distant mountains. The lake was frozen and everything was just white. In his opinion, it looked better in the spring.

Suddenly everything turned dark. It was night. Mike was not able to understand. Why did everything turn dark? The day just disappeared and the night replaced it.

Mike saw a man ahead of him. The man was standing there, looking at everything. He did not know that someone was behind him.

Mike wanted to say something to the man, but he realized that he was not controlling himself. Something else was. He crept up behind the man and put his arm around his throat. The man began to choke. He struggled his way out of Mike's grip but he was not able to free himself.

Soon Mike put his hand over the man's throat and ripped it out. He let go and the man fell to the ground.

Mike stood over the lifeless body. He did not know why he just killed the man. He did not want to. Now he had blood on his hands. He was guilty of murder.

Mike quickly sat up in bed. He looked around and saw that it was dark. He looked at the time and saw that it was one in the morning. He had been sleeping the entire time. It was only a dream.

Mike caught his breath. He was glad that he was only dreaming. Why did he dream of such a violent thing? He dreamt of killing a man. Why was that?

It was strange that Jon mentioned the killer earlier in the day and that was when Mike had the dream. "I've never had a dream like that since the first day I could remember. Why did I have it now?"

Mike tried to get the nightmare out of his head but he was not able to. It was bothering him. He killed someone in his mental images. He wondered why such a thing would even enter his head. He thought that it was probably because the killer was mentioned earlier.

"But why would *I* be the one killing?" Mike asked himself. He was not able to get over it. He did not get sleep for the rest of the night.

The following morning Mike was driving to the police station. He was very tired for the reason that he did not get much rest the preceding night. He had just finished drinking coffee so that he would not fall asleep at the wheel.

Mike soon saw a familiar face entering a truck. He saw that the person had a pack of beer in his hand. He put the pack on the passenger seat and then he entered the car.

Mike drove over to the truck before the man drove away. He pulled over behind the vehicle. The driver noticed that a police car was behind him so he did not drive away. He just sighed and slammed his hand on the steering wheel.

Mike stepped out of his car and walked over to the truck. The driver lowered his window and asked, "What did I do?" He looked at whom he was talking to. "You again?"

"Stay in the car," Mike said. "I'm going to go check if your license is still suspended because I have doubts."

"It ain't suspended."

"I'll go find that out."

Mike walked back to his car and entered it. He had to find out if this driver was allowed to drive yet.

Soon Mike came back over to the driver. "I hope you know that your license was suspended that other day for two weeks. Those two weeks have not passed by yet."

"Ah, come on. Just give me a break and go away. It's not like I'm gonna hurt somebody."

"I'm afraid that I'm going to have to take you to jail, sir."

"There's no way in hell that I'm gonna go to jail."

"Please step out of the car."

"Hell no. You ain't takin' me nowhere." The driver crossed his arms.

"I'm being very patient with you, sir. Don't make me repeat it again. Step out of the car."

The driver refused to cooperate.

Mike opened the door and started to pull the driver out. The man fought back. He was trying to get Mike away from him.

Eventually Mike pulled the driver out. "Now put your hands behind your back."

The driver did that. He was no longer going to fight back. He knew that he was not going to win.

Mike placed a pair of handcuffs over the man's hands and walked with him over to the police car. He placed the man in there and shut the door. Then he contacted a tow company to take the car away.

Mike arrived at the police station after everything was over with. He walked up to Jon and Susan. He greeted them and they greeted him back.

"Jon, do you remember that drunk guy that we caught?" Mike asked.

"Yes," answered Jon.

"I saw him driving again and noticed that his license was suspended. I had to go take him to jail."

"I knew that you were going to be a good officer."

Mike changed the subject. "And you'll never believe what happened to me last night."

"I'll be back, Mike," said Jon. "Someone's calling me."

Mike faced Susan and began to speak. "I'll tell him later. Anyway, I had this really strange dream. I was at that place behind my house. The place that I took you, remember?"

Susan nodded.

"Well, it started off there. I was looking at the snowy scene. It was cool. Then all of a sudden, everything went black. It gets even stranger. I saw this man ahead of me. I don't where he came from. He was just standing there. I sneaked up behind him and put my arm around his neck. He tried to fight back, but I had him in a good grip. I put my hand on his throat and tore it apart. I killed him."

"Why would you kill him?"

"I don't know. That's the thing. I guess it's because Jon was talking about the killer yesterday."

"So in your dream, you played the killer? That's really odd."

"I know. I don't know why it took place there of all places."

"Mike, it's just a dream. You'll get over it soon. It was only a figment of your imagination."

Mike changed the subject again. "I'm going to move out of that house anyway. I know where I'm going to move. I saw this house about five minutes away from here. It was actually pretty nice. Nobody lived in there. That's the place I'm going to live in."

That was when Jon arrived. "All right," he said to Mike, "I heard you say that you're moving."

"I am. I found the right house. I'm packing my things up in two days."

"So no more abandoned house."

"Nope. That's it for that small house."

"I would get tired of living there, too. It's so hard to find. It's so far from everyone. I've always wondered why you lived in such a mysterious place."

"I've always been wondering that, too."

Jon was now confused. "Now why is it that *you've* been wondering? Didn't you move there?"

Mike was thinking of an answer. He started to speak. "As a matter of fact, I don't remember moving into the house because my family moved in there when I was just born."

"Didn't you grow up there then?"

"I lived at my uncle's house with my cousin because my parents were very abusive. My cousin found that out and secretly took me to his house when I was like a year and a half."

"How did you figure out where you actually lived and why did you go back?"

"You ask a lot of questions, don't you, Jon?" Susan said.

Mike was glad she interrupted because he did not want to keep thinking of answers. "Yeah, that's true," he said. "You're very inquisitive."

"No, I just thought it was interesting," Jon replied.

"Well, we better get to work. We can't waste time here talking."

Later, as soon as Jon and Susan left, Mike thought for a moment. The questions that Jon asked him made him think about many things. Why *did* he live in such a solitary place?

"I wonder if I still have that envelope that the doctor found," Mike said quietly to himself. "Maybe it belonged to somebody I knew. Perhaps they can give me answers."

Right when Mike arrived home, he began to search for the envelope. He searched through his drawers and his closet. Eventually he found it.

"Here it is," said Mike as he sat on his bed. He lifted up the flap of the envelope and saw a letter inside. He pulled it out. It read:

"Hey, Mike. Meet me at my place. George Benson." The man's address was at the bottom of the letter.

Mike put the letter back into the envelope and began to ponder for a moment. "Did he send the letter to me or was it someone I knew? I wonder if my name is actually Mike."

Later Mike was standing in front of the man's house. It took him an hour to walk there. He walked up the pathway and knocked on the door. He knocked twice before a middle-aged man answered it.

"Are you George Benson?" Mike asked.

"I could be," the man replied. "It all depends on who you are and what you want."

"I'm just here to ask him a few questions."

"Well, George can't answer questions right now. I'm not George. He's in the shower."

Before the man closed the door, Mike said, "I just need to know if he knew Mike Riley."

The man turned to Mike and stuck out his hand. "Hi. I'm George Benson. Who are you?"

Mike shook his hand. "It doesn't matter who I am now. May I please come in?"

The man stepped away from the doorway. "Yeah," he answered. "Sure. Come on in."

Mike entered the house and the man closed the door behind him.

"Here," said the man as he gestured toward the chairs that were in the living room. "Have a seat. Do you want a drink or anything?"

"No, thanks," responded Mike.

The man sat down across from Mike. "So what is it that you need to talk to me about? You said something about Mike Riley."

"Yeah." Mike reached into his pocket and pulled out the envelope. "You sent this to him, right?" He handed the letter to the man.

The man took the letter from Mike. "Yeah, I sent this to him a long time ago. He never showed up."

"What happened to him?"

"I don't know. About two days later, I went over to his house and no one was there. I never saw him since then." The man looked at Mike weirdly and asked, "How did you get this letter?"

"I don't know. That's why I'm here. I need to know something. Have you ever seen me before?"

The man shook his head.

"I don't look familiar to you in any way? Have you ever seen me around Mike?"

"No, I haven't. How did you get the letter? I gave it to Mike."

Mike hesitated for a moment. In order to get an answer, he was going to have to tell the man the truth. He said, "I woke up in this bed about a few months ago. This doctor was there and he found the envelope next to this bag I had. He said that possibly my name was Mike Riley because I didn't know what my name was. I still don't know what it actually is. I don't recollect any detail about my past."

"Really?" the man asked surprisingly. "That's strange. Maybe Mike *did* know you and he possibly gave it to you so you could hold on to it or something—I don't know. I don't see any other way that you could have possibly gotten it."

"Neither do I. See? I came to you to see if you could help me with my past because I thought that you were a relative of mine. Now I see that you're not and that my name isn't really Mike."

"So now you're going under that name?"

"Yeah. I have a completely different identity though. It's a long story of how I got it so I won't get into that."

"You don't have any parents or siblings or cousins or friends that can help you?"

Mike shook his head. "No. I was lucky to have my address written on that suitcase that day I woke up. I went over to my house and found out that no one else lived with me and I didn't have any pictures of anyone."

"That must be really strange. You don't have anything?"

"I hardly had anything in that house. It was filthy and nearly empty. I don't know how I was able to manage. There was no food in the refrigerator or on the counters."

"Wow," said the man. "You led a mysterious life. How can you not have someone that recognizes you? I actually find that amazing and very interesting."

"I guess *you* can say that. I find it very disturbing. It's driving me crazy. I really want to know who I was in the past."

"Maybe you were a survivor of a natural disaster that killed your entire family. You never know."

"That's true," Mike said as he thought about that. That could have been a possibility.

The telephone began to ring. The man stood up and said, "Excuse me." He walked over to the telephone and picked it up. He answered it.

Mike sat there and stared at the goldfish that were inside a large tank ahead of him. They were huge goldfish. They were not even swimming—they were more or less floating. The smallest one was the only one that was swimming. It swam around the bigger fish a few times. Then it started to shove itself through the small rocks at the bottom of the tank. It swam away from there and went through a castle that was built inside the tank. It went back into the castle and stayed inside there. That was the place that it decided to stay in.

Mike was thinking that he possibly did not even have a place to stay in. He had no one to get in contact with. He did not have anyone to tell him who he was in the past or what he liked to do. He looked around the place and saw many pictures. He saw one picture of a small boy fishing with a man. Mike figured that that was George because there was a slight resemblance.

Mike sighed. It was a shame that he did not have any pictures of himself as a boy. He did not have one picture of anything.

Soon Mike heard the telephone slam down. He looked away from the fish tank.

George walked over to Mike and said, "Sorry about that."

"It's okay," Mike replied. "I'm on my way anyway."

"Really? You don't need to say anything else?"

"No. That's all. It was nice talking to you." Mike extended his arm.

George shook Mike's hand and responded, "It was nice speaking to you, too. I hope you find answers about your past."

"Thanks."

Soon Mike was outside George's home. He was ready for the long walk ahead of him.

Mike turned to his right and began walking down the sidewalk. He saw a red convertible sports car stop in front of the house across the street. Teens were riding inside the car and they had the music blasting. Two teenage girls entered the car and they drove off.

Mike continued walking down the sidewalk. He was looking up ahead of him as the sun was starting to set. It made a beautiful orange and pinkish color to the sky. It was a nice sight.

Another thing that was ahead of Mike was a man riding a bicycle. The man was riding toward him so he moved over to the side so that he would not be in the man's way. The man rode by and Mike continued walking.

Soon Mike sat down on a bench. He decided to stay there awhile since he was not in a rush to go to his lonely cottage. He was not going to do anything there so he might as well sit down and enjoy the outdoors in the city.

A black stray cat jumped on the bench next to Mike. The cat stood there and stared up at Mike. It walked a little closer to him.

"Go on," Mike said as he motioned it to go away. "Go on home or wherever you live. I don't keep pets—they're too messy."

The cat, of course not understanding, stayed there. It stared at Mike with its blue-grayish eyes. It then meowed.

Mike figured that it wanted something. "I don't have any food."

The cat meowed again.

"I don't have any yarn, either. I don't have anything that you might want. Why don't you run along and crash into a person that has something?"

The cat sat down and stared straight at Mike.

Mike stood up. He looked down at the cat and then walked away. He stood at the end of the sidewalk and looked to his left. A car was coming. It stopped at the stop sign and after that, it made a right turn and drove away.

When Mike noticed that no automobiles were coming, he crossed the road and kept on walking down the next sidewalk.

Mike heard a low noise behind him while he was walking. He turned around and saw nothing. When he looked down, he saw the black cat again. It was following him.

Mike faced forward. "Why is this cat following me?" he asked himself. He continued walking.

Soon the cat ran into an alley. There were plenty of garbage cans there. The cat knocked one over and began eating the garbage out of the can.

Mike was glad that the cat found food. Now he did not need to worry about it following him around anymore.

The sun was almost gone and it was really beginning to darken. Mike had been walking for nearly half an hour. He knew that he needed to walk halfway more.

Mike heard a low noise behind him again. He turned around and looked down. The black cat was back.

"Why are you following me?" Mike asked the cat as if it would answer. "Why don't you go someplace else? I'm not the perfect guy to follow around."

Mike turned forward and continued his walk. He was hoping that the cat would go away before he arrived home. He was thinking that it would.

There was a record store ahead. A man was closing it for the day. Mike passed by the store. Right next to the store was a barbershop. It was still open and man was getting his hair cut.

Mike turned around to see if the cat was still there and it was. He turned forward and continued walking. He walked by a high school where many shootings occurred. It was a very old school and it had always been the site where many deaths occurred.

Later Mike walked in complete darkness. He was barely able to see anything. He was away from the city and the only things that surrounded him now were trees. The moon did not shine through them because there were so many. That was why there was hardly any light at all. It was also a very quiet place to walk.

Mike had walked in that place in the dark before. The first time he did, he was not able to tell where he was going. Many branches had scratched him because he had headed in the wrong direction. He actually got lost. He slept next to a tree until sunup. That was when he had found his way back.

Now Mike was able to walk in the dark without a problem. He was not able to see many things but he eventually got accustomed to it.

Fifteen minutes later Mike was finally home. He grabbed his house key that was in the right pocket of his jacket. He stuck it inside the keyhole of the doorknob and turned it. The door was opened and he put the key back in his pocket. He opened the door and stepped inside. He turned the light on and there he saw the black cat on top of the desk in front of him.

"Where did you come from?" Mike asked as he turned around and faced outside since the door was still open behind him. "I thought that you stopped following me. How did you get inside here?"

Mike was about to grab the cat and place it outside but something came to him. It seemed like a flashback. He saw images everywhere. He saw a glass of wine crash to the ground with a hand right next to it. Then he saw a black cat trying to escape. The next thing that he saw was the cat fall dead on the ground after its head had been cut off.

Mike wiped the images out of his mind. He looked over at the desk again and the cat was gone. He found this really strange now. He closed the door and began to search for the cat. He was thinking that it probably jumped off of the desk and made its way around the house.

Mike searched under the desk. He stood up and began to look everywhere. He called for the cat and saw that there was no sign of it.

"Maybe it's in my room," Mike said to himself. He walked down the hallway and went into his bedroom. He always left the door open and that was why he thought that the animal could have been inside there.

Mike searched his room and there was no sign of the cat. There was no sign of it anywhere. It was not in the house.

Mike sat on his bed. "I've heard that if you see a black cat too many times, it could bring you misfortune. But of course I don't believe that because I don't follow those superstitious things."

Mike lied back on his bed. "Well, at least that cat's over with," he said. "I better get some rest."

Mike stood up and turned off all the lights in the house. He went back into his bedroom and turned the lamp off. Then he went onto his bed and started to fall asleep.

The next morning started off with a huge snowstorm. It was not a nice morning after all. There were harsh winds blowing and snow was falling down. Many people had to stay inside buildings and wait for the storm to die down. It eventually did two hours later.

After the snowstorm was over, it left behind a huge sheet of snow. It was about twenty-five inches deep. A number of people were not able to drive home. They had to wait for workers to scoop the snow off the streets.

It took quite a while for them to do that.

Jon was in his house slowly stroking his dog's fur. He had to bring the dog inside because of the storm. He did not do anything but sit there with the dog.

Soon Jon heard the front door slam behind him. He did not really pay attention to it. He was busy thinking about different things.

A voice said, "Didn't expect the storm, huh?"

Jon turned around and saw his brother. "I didn't expect you back so early."

Will took his leather jacket off and placed it over a chair. He sat down on a chair and said, "All I did was talk to the guy."

"And how'd it go?"

It took a short while for Will to answer. He soon said, "It wasn't him. You were right."

"How do you know?"

"I asked him some questions. He told me that he lied about ever coming here. He has never even been here. He did that because he wanted us to stop frantically searching for the criminal. I knew it wasn't him just by looking at him."

"How'd you know that he wasn't lying about not being the killer?"

"I had doubts when I first looked at him. Since I did, I went over to question him. I asked him why he gunned down dad. He said because he wanted to feel proud. At that moment I knew that he wasn't the killer because we both know that dad was not gunned down."

Jon let his dog wander around the house. "I told you," he said. "I knew that it wasn't going to be the killer. You didn't want to believe me. I knew that they didn't find him. It seemed too odd."

"I know. The reason I went was because I wanted to take any chance that I had. I wanted to take every opportunity that I was able to get. I really want to catch that criminal."

"I'm sure we will."

Will stood up and went into the kitchen. From there he shouted, "I saw this movie on the plane about some killer that the law was after. It kind of reminded me of us." He began to make himself some coffee. "The killer always killed in the dark and the way he killed was by tricking people into helping him. Well, later on he died. Some guy killed him. After that, the guy killed himself. The police didn't know that so they kept on searching for the killer. The movie ended off when an officer said, 'Don't worry. We'll find him.' It was a strange movie."

"The killer we're looking for could possible by dead, too," Jon said.

"I knew you were going to say that. That's why I told you about the movie."

"No. It could possibly be true. What if the killer killed himself to escape all of these punishments? You never know. He could be dead and we're searching for someone we'll never find."

Will came out of the kitchen. "Well, we'll need to make sure of that. We'll have to find out somehow if he really did die."

"That's why we're not hearing anything on him anymore. There aren't anymore killings done by him. He could be dead."

"Or he could be in another country. He probably decided to leave."

"I don't know. Maybe he did. We'll find out someday."

For the first time in a while, Will smiled. "I knew that movie was going to get to you. It was going to make you think things over." He reentered the kitchen.

Jon stood up. He was going to feed his dog. "You're right," he said. "That movie *did* make me think things over. That's a good thing, though." He grabbed the bag of dog food. He unrolled the bag and poured the dog food inside the bowl. He rolled it back up and called the dog. The dog came in no time. It then began eating the food.

Jon placed the dog food back where he found it. "I'm going to leave soon," he suddenly said.

Will came out of the kitchen with a mug of coffee in his hand. "In this weather?" he asked. He took a sip from the coffee.

"It's not so bad now. It was worse previously. I think I'll be able to manage. I've driven in this before."

"It's pretty early."

"I know. The earlier I go the better. I'm going to go get dressed."

Jon went down the hallway and into his room. Will sat down and drank his cup of coffee.

Mike was in his bedroom packing all of his clothes away. He had two suitcases on his bed and he was putting his clothes inside of them. He was getting ready to move out. He was going to move in his new home the in a few days. He wanted to get things over with.

Soon Mike heard a knock at the front door. He wondered who it could have possibly been. He walked to the front door and opened it. He saw Jon there.

"Hey, Mike," greeted Jon.

"Hi, Jon," Mike said back. "I'm stunned to see you here." He removed himself from the doorway so that Jon would step inside the house.

Jon stepped inside and said, "I came here to help you pack your things up. You said that you were going to do it a few days ago."

Mike closed the door. "You don't have to help me, Jon. I mean, don't waste your time."

"It's not a waste of time. I have nothing better to do anyway."

Mike did not say anything for a moment. He broke the silence by asking, "So did Will come back yet?"

"Yes, he did," answered Jon.

"What happened?"

"With our luck, it wasn't the killer. I had a feeling that it wasn't him from the start."

"You think *you* have bad luck? Guess what happened to me last night."

"What?"

"Some black cat kept on following me last night. It followed me all the way here. At first, I thought that it was gone once I left the city. Then I came inside here, turned on the light, and saw it on top of there." He pointed towards the desk.

"Really? That must have been strange."

"That's not the end of it. I was about to go over to it and put it outside, but some weird pictures went into my head. I saw some woman fall with a glass of wine in her hand. The next thing that was in my head was a cat trying to run away from something or someone. Next thing you know, the cat dies because its head gets cut off."

"All that was in your head? That's crazy."

"That's still not the end of it. When I looked over at the table again, the cat was gone. I looked everywhere around this house and the cat was nowhere to be found. I figured that it probably left, but why would it all of a sudden leave after following me around for so long? I found that strange."

"That's one of the strangest things that I've heard. Why would you get those pictures in your head?"

"I don't know," Mike answered as he went inside the kitchen. Jon followed him. "I've been hallucinating from time to time now. I get these strange pictures in my head. You know what's funny?"

"What?"

"All the pictures are about something or someone being killed. They're all violent images." Mike opened up a cabinet and pulled out a barrel of Pringles. "I still don't understand why I'm getting them."

"Maybe you should see a psychologist or something. That's not something normal."

"I know." Mike opened up the barrel. He pulled out a few chips. "Want some?"

"No, thanks," Jon answered. "I was in eighth grade the last time I had those. I stopped eating them because they made my lips bleed."

Mike put the barrel away. He ate one of the chips that were in his hand. "They made your lips bleed?" he asked. "How can Pringles make your lips bleed?"

"I don't know," Jon responded. "I went to the doctor to see if anything was wrong with me. He said that I was perfectly normal. He also told me never to eat Pringles for a while. I just totally stopped eating them."

Mike ate another chip. "How do you know if they still make your lips bleed?"

"I don't know if they do. I don't want to take anymore chances."

"You were in eighth grade, Jon. How do you know if that still could happen to you? Maybe you got over it."

"Mike, if someone wasn't able to make a three-point shot in basketball when he or she was in the eighth grade and that person stopped trying until now, do you think that he or she would be able to do it now?"

"It could be a possibility. Some people would be able to do it."

"But without practicing? How can that person suddenly make it?"

"That's different though. I mean...I don't know. I'm just thinking that maybe you won't have such an allergic reaction to these anymore."

"Didn't something strange like that happen to you when you were younger?"

Mike did not answer. He was thinking of an answer.

"Mike?"

"What?" Mike answered. "I wasn't really paying attention to your question. What did you say?"

"I asked if something strange ever happened to you when you were younger."

"Umm...I don't recall anything like that happening. I can barely remember anything that happened back then."

"Why?"

"Because it all went by so quick. Time really does fly by like wind. It goes by so fast. I can remember my first day seeing the world as if it were yesterday."

"You remember that clearly?"

"Yeah. It wasn't so long ago."

"Sometimes I wonder about you, Mike. You say the strangest things. When I talk to you about past life, you start to say weird things."

"That's the way I am," Mike responded. "I was always like that."

Jon looked around the house. "Sometimes this place reminds me of something that happened long ago."

"What?"

"It makes me think that this is the place where…" Jon stopped. He looked at Mike and said, "Never mind."

"What? What does it make you think?"

"It's nothing important. I was just thinking about something that happened to a place similar to this one."

"What happened?"

That was when both men heard a loud noise outside. "What was that?" Jon asked.

"I don't know," answered Mike. "Let's go find out."

Mike walked over to the front door and Jon followed him. He opened the door and saw a buck trying to free its right hind leg from a deep hole in the ground. It was moving very wildly.

"Poor guy is stuck," Mike said.

"You're going to try to help that?" Jon asked as he watched the buck go wild.

"Yeah. If I don't do anything about it, no one else will and that thing is going to stay there forever. Either that, or it'll walk around with three legs."

"How are you going to help it?"

"Come with me."

Mike walked over to the buck. The animal looked at him and made strange noises. It went even wilder.

"How are you going to help that thing?" Jon asked as he backed away.

"Calm it down for me."

"How?"

"Hold on. I'll be right back."

Mike went inside his house and went straight to the refrigerator. He opened it and pulled out a bag of carrots. He grabbed a carrot and closed the door. He went back out the front door.

Mike handed Jon the carrot. "Give this to the buck," he said.

Jon took the carrot. "I'll try."

"That's the only thing that'll calm it down for a while."

Jon showed the carrot to the buck. The animal stopped moving as soon as it saw the food.

Jon placed the carrot toward the buck's mouth and the animal began to eat it.

While Jon was doing that, Mike was busy pulling the animal's leg out. He had to do it slowly and carefully. The hole was very deep.

The buck was soon finished with the carrot. At the same time, its leg was free. It was able to run off into the trees.

"Good job, Mike," Jon commented. He was very surprised.

Mike stood up. "It's not the first time that I deal with stuff like that."

"Really?"

"Yes, really. I helped this rabbit free itself from a trap that some-one put on the ground. I helped a deer get its head out of a log. I even helped a bear before. It was tangled in many ropes. I helped it free itself."

"How'd you do that?"

"That one's a long story. Just put it this way—I made the bear free. It looked at me for a quick moment and then it ran off when I freed it."

"How big was it?"

"It was huge. It was a giant grizzly."

Jon did not say anything. He was surprised at how Mike was able to do so many things.

"Let's go back inside," Mike said.

"Yeah," Jon agreed. "Aren't you going to pack your things?"

"Yeah. Let's do that very quickly. I don't have many things to pack up anyway. I don't have much stuff."

Mike and Jon went inside the cottage. They both went inside Mike's room.

"I'm almost done with everything," Mike said. "I just need a cou-ple of more clothes and I'm done."

Jon did not say anything. He looked around the room.

Mike was pulling clothes out of his closet and putting them inside the suitcase. He looked at Jon who was thinking pensively. He smiled and said, "What's wrong with you? You like my room?"

"I'm just thinking. I'll help you put some stuff away."

Before Jon did that, he saw something that caught his eye. It was on top of Mike's bed. He saw a dark coat and dark pants. He stared at that for a moment.

Jon then asked, "Where did you get those clothes?"

"What?" Mike questioned as he turned around.

"Those black clothes that are on your bed."

Mike picked the coat up. "This? I don't know where I got this. I found it in my suitcase a long time ago. I don't know where it came from. I just decided to put it away for a while. I've never worn it.' He placed it back down and went back over to his closet.

"Are you sure you don't know where you got it?"

"I'm sure."

Something was coming to Jon. He had to check. He picked the coat up and looked at the back of it. He saw a rip there. He was thinking of the time when he was looking at the tape and he saw the killer's coat rip through the door because it got stuck.

So far Jon was not able to believe what he was seeing. "Do you know how the coat ripped?" he asked.

"No," Mike answered as he put more clothing inside his suitcase. "It was already like that when I first saw it." He went back into the closet.

Jon put the coat down. He decided to look at the pants. They were the last things that he was going to look at. He grabbed the pants and searched inside the left pocket. There was nothing inside. He then searched inside the right pocket and felt a piece of paper in there. He pulled out the paper and looked at it. It was folded. He unfolded it and saw that it was his father's form. He was extremely shocked.

"How did you get this?" Jon asked with a less friendly tone in his voice.

"What?" Mike asked as he looked over. "What is that?"

"You should know. It was in your pockets."

"I don't know. I don't even wear those clothes anymore. That was probably already in there."

"How did you get these clothes? Did they just appear there? You're lying, Mike."

"Jon, what's your problem? What are you talking about?"

"Those are your clothes and this form was inside the pants."

"What form is that? Jon, you're making me feel nervous."

"You should be nervous. After all of this time of searching, I have finally found him."

Mike was extremely confused. "Jon, what are you talking about?" he asked calmly.

John spoke a bit calmly as well. "It's you, Mike. I can't believe this."

"What? What do you mean *it's you*?"

"It's you," Jon repeated. "You're the killer."

CHAPTER 6

❀

MIKE LOOKED AT JON WITH DAZEDNESS. HE DID NOT UNDERSTAND A THING HIS friend was saying. "What do you mean I'm the killer?" he questioned.

"You know very well what I mean," Jon told him. "You were the killer the whole time and we didn't even know it. Was this your only way to escape from getting captured?"

"Jon, you're going crazy. I'm not the killer."

"Of course you'd say that now, Mike Riley. That's why you were always acting weird when I asked you questions about your past. You had no way to answer them."

"No. It isn't that."

"Then what is it?" Jon looked around the room. "And this place—it *does* remind me of something. I think this is the place I'm thinking of." He left the room.

Mike followed him. "Wait, Jon," he called. "Where are you going?"

Jon did not answer. He went out the front door. He walked behind the house and through the trees. It took him a short while to finally arrive at the scene that was behind the cottage. Again, he was surprised.

"I was right," said Jon as he looked around. "This is it. This is where it happened. I knew it."

Mike, who had been following Jon all along, stopped walking and asked, "What happened here? What are you talking about?"

"You should know. This is where some innocent man died. He was standing here doing nothing but looking at this place. You then came over to him secretly and slit his throat with a sharp blade."

"I did?" Mike asked as he began to think. Something came to him.

"No. No, this can't be happening." He covered half his face with his hand. "This can't be."

"What?" Jon asked as he looked over at him. "What can't be?"

Mike removed his hand from his face. "I should have told you a long time ago, Jon."

"What?"

"That's why I've been having violent images."

"Because you're the killer—that's why. You can't escape anymore. You're going to prison."

"I can explain everything," a voice said.

Mike and Jon both looked to their right. A man was standing there.

"Who are you?" questioned Jon.

"I am the one that found Mr. Riley lying unconscious next to a destroyed building."

"How did you get here?" Mike asked.

"I drove to a place that was nearby your home after I dropped you off at the bus stop. I've been living in a small cabin about a few minutes away from here. I've been waiting until something like this came up."

The doctor then continued with his story. "Anyway, I brought him to my office. By the way, I'm a doctor. He woke up hours later and he did not even know who he was or where he came from."

"So what are you trying to say?" Jon asked.

"What I'm trying to tell you is that he suffers from amnesia."

Jon was extremely stunned. He could have never imagined that Mike suffered from amnesia.

Jon began to speak. "So that means that—"

"I was a killer in my past life," Mike finished off for him. He was speaking very softly. "Now I know the answer."

"I never dealt with something like this," Jon explained. "I don't know what to do or say."

The doctor began to speak. "He got the name Mike Riley from an envelope that I found on his suitcase."

Jon kept quiet.

"I know the perfect person to speak to," Mike stated.

Jon and the doctor did not say anything. They just waited for Mike to say the name.

Mike then said, "George Benson."

Jon drove Mike to George's house. The doctor stayed behind and went back to his cabin. He wished Mike the best of luck.

Jon and Mike arrived at George's house. They stepped out of the car and walked up the pathway. When they arrived at the door, Mike rang the doorbell.

George answered it in no time. "Why, hello," he greeted Mike. "It's nice to see you around here again."

"Hi," said Mike. He gestured toward Jon. "This is my friend, Jon. We need to ask you some questions."

"Sure. Come on in."

Mike and Jon entered the house. George closed the door behind him and offered his visitors a drink, but they did not want anything at the time.

George sat at a table. He was across from Jon and diagonally from Mike. He asked, "So what is it that you guys need to talk to me about?"

Jon questioned, "From what I've heard, you knew the real Mike Riley, right?"

George nodded. "Right."

"Do you know what happened to him?"

"No. I was supposed to meet him somewhere and he never showed up. I went over to his house later and saw that no one was there—not even his wife."

Jon thought for a moment. The next question he asked was, "Did he live in a somewhat huge house?"

"Yes."

"Did he have a fence that had a guard dog sign but there was actually no dog there?"

"Yes."

"I know who you're talking about."

"How do you know?"

"I'm an officer. I worked on that case."

George was anxious for an answer to his question. "What happened to him?"

"We found him dead when we arrived there. A neighbor of his called us over there. His wife committed suicide after she found out that her husband died. A murderer killed him."

"Me," Mike said lowly, nearly in a whisper. "I killed him. I can't believe this."

George looked over at Mike. "You killed him?"

Mike looked up at George. "I was the famous killer in the past. I finally found that out today. I was a killer."

"A killer?" George asked, surprised. "That is so weird." He looked over at Jon. "What are you going to do about that?"

"I don't know," Jon answered. "This is the strangest case I've ever dealt with. Once we arrested this man for killing his sister. We later found out that he had mental disorders."

"Really?"

Jon nodded. "We had to keep him there for a while. That case wasn't nearly as strange as this one."

"It must be hard to be an officer."

Jon said nothing. Neither did Mike.

Soon Jon stood up. "Well, I guess that's all we came here for," he said.

"That's all?" George asked. He stood up as well. "That was a quick talk."

"Yeah, I know."

Mike stood up from his chair. "Goodbye, George," he said.

George said goodbye to both of the men. Before they went out the door, he said, "Thanks for telling me what happened to my pal."

"Anytime," Jon said over his shoulder. He and Mike walked over to his car.

Mike and Jon were back at the cottage. Jon had the driver's door opened and he stood right next to it. He had his arms on the top of the car. He said, "Well, Mike, I wouldn't worry much if I were you."

Mike turned to him. "Why?"

"Because I consider you innocent. I don't think that you should be arrested."

"Yeah, but what would the others think? They're not going to take this the way you are. What's your brother going to think?"

"I'm sure that there's a way to get him to think the right way. I can convince him somehow."

"Are you sure about that?"

"Of course. I've lived with him for years. There's probably a way to convince him."

"Okay," said Mike. "I hope you're right."

"I'll see you soon, Mike."

"Bye, Jon."

Mike turned around and walked to his home. He opened the door and entered it. Then he closed the door behind him.

Jon entered his car and started it up. After that he drove off.

While Jon was driving to his house, he began to doubt himself. He was starting to think that there was no way to make Will think the same way he did. He was trying to think of the many ways that he could possibly convince his brother.

There was plenty of traffic. The sounds of horns were able to be heard everywhere. There had never been that many cars in the wintertime.

Jon stopped at a stoplight. A car pulled up next to him. Very loud music was being played from the car. The people in the cars around it were able to feel the vibrations of the song. It was deafening.

Jon was not able to think because of the car beside him. He was wondering how the driver was able to tolerate music that loud. The driver was probably going to get his hearing impaired anyway.

Jon looked over at the car next to him with the loud music. He glanced at the driver. The driver was a young man, maybe in his late teens, with a sleeveless white shirt on and dark hair. The window on his side was lowered down and he rested his left arm there. His hand was on the steering wheel. He was leaned back against his chair and he was moving his head to the beat of the song.

Jon turned away from the driver and looked ahead. He saw the light finally turn green. He continued to drive again.

The driver with the loud music was going the same way as Jon. Jon still had to put up with the music. He looked over at the car with the music and saw it make a left turn. It was gone at last.

Jon was glad that he was away from the driver. Loud music always ruined his concentration. That very moment was the worst time to ruin his concentration.

Jon finally arrived home after a long drive. He exited his car and walked to the front door. He grabbed his keys and unlocked the door. He stepped inside the house and closed the door.

The first thing Jon saw was Will talking on the telephone. He was speaking about a meeting.

"Yes," Will said on the receiver. "I'll be there right away. It'll take me fifteen minutes." He paused for a moment. After the pause, he continued. "I will surely be there."

Jon tried to speak to his brother. He was saying, "I need to speak to you." He was saying that inaudibly.

Will looked at him and mouthed "not now". He kept on speaking. "I will not miss this meeting."

"I need to talk to you about the killer," Jon said.

"Cancel the meeting," Will said as soon as he heard his brother. "I'm sorry. It will have to be another day." He paused and then he continued speaking. "That's okay. Thank you. Goodbye." He hung up the telephone and faced Jon.

"Who were you talking to?" Jon asked.

"Some woman that needs to speak to me," Will answered. "Now what about the killer?"

"Well," Jon started. "The reason why that guy wasn't the killer was because...the actual killer is around here and I know who it is."

Will was not able to believe what he was hearing. "Are you sure you know?"

"Yes."

"How?"

"I went to someone's house and I saw the same exact clothes that the killer wore. The same dark coat that the killer wore was there and it was ripped just like we saw on the videotape. I looked in the pockets of the pants and found the letter that the killer put inside there. It was a form of dad's."

"So who's the killer?"

"The killer was someone that we knew all along...Mike."

"Mike?"

"Yes. I couldn't believe it, either. I thought that it was incredible."

"I knew that there was something wrong with him. He tried to trick us."

"No, he didn't. He's not a killer anymore."

"What do you mean he's not a killer anymore?"

"He doesn't remember anything about killing. He has no memories of his past life."

"Past life? He has amnesia?"

"Yes."

"How do you know this?"

"Some doctor told me that."

Will shook his head. "That doctor's probably playing in Mike's little game as well. He's probably an assistant."

"No, he's not."

"You believe everything they tell you, don't you? Mike's the killer and now he's going to prison for it. That's the bottom line."

"Mike doesn't remember anything about being a murderer," Jon argued.

"He's probably pretending to have amnesia to escape from going to prison. That's a nice trick. We're probably his next victims."

"How can we be his next victims if he's not a killer anymore?"

"He probably is. You don't know that for sure."

Jon sighed. "Will, the man has amnesia."

"Okay. I don't care if he does or if he doesn't. He's still going to be detained."

"Why are you arresting him if he doesn't know anything about killing anyone?"

"He killed our father. I've always wanted the killer to be placed in prison."

"But it's like he's already in prison because he's not doing harm to anyone anymore."

That did not make Will change his mind. He still argued back. "No, he's going to prison one way or another. I can't walk around knowing that he killed dad. I want to see him being tortured for what he did."

"Tortured? Will, come on. It's like doing that to an innocent man."

"No, it isn't. He's the killer and he's going to pay for what he's done. He's not escaping this time."

"Wouldn't it be better if you tortured the actual killer?"

Will did a short laugh. "Who is the actual killer to you?"

"The other Mike."

"The other Mike. To you, that's what he is. To me, he's still the same. One way or another, he's being arrested."

"Can you listen to me for once? Don't do this."

"Why should I listen to you? You're always thinking to do the stupid things. You make the worst decisions. I'm going with what's right."

"Taking an innocent man to jail isn't right."

"Innocent man?" Will exclaimed. "Is that how much you care about dad? You think that his killer is an innocent man? I knew that I would have to handle this case alone."

"Will, stop being so…"

"No. Let's end this right here. He's being arrested one way or another. I don't care if you help or not. I'll do it myself if I have to."

"Can you please…?"

"You're not going to change my mind, so you might as well just not say anything else. Mike is going to be turned in and he's going to prison."

"If you were a lawyer, you'd probably argue until you knew he was going to go to jail."

"Damn right I would. I should have become a prosecutor."

"You'd be good at it. Nothing can change your mind."

"I've waited so long to see this killer being tortured," Will said coldly. "He's going to deserve it for what he did."

Jon shook his head. "I don't know what to say anymore."

"That's good. Don't say anything."

Will was about to go to into the hallway, but Jon stopped him by asking, "Would you be saying this right now if you found out *I* was the killer?" He asked that question because he knew that Will did not like Mike from the start. He wanted to see if that was the reason why he wanted to turn him in.

Will turned to him and answered, "Yes, I would. I would want you to go to prison. It doesn't matter that you're my brother. You should treat a certain person like you would treat anyone else. I'm not going to take someone to prison just because I don't know him or her. Just because you're my brother doesn't mean that I won't treat you like a regular suspect. If you want to be a criminal, then you'll be treated like a criminal."

"Really?"

"Yes, really. What—you wouldn't turn me in if I committed a crime?"

"I don't know. It *would* be kind of hard."

"Hard? Is that why you're defending Mike so much—because he's your friend? You should learn to have a strong mind and accept what's right. You should know what's right to be done."

"It's not that," Jon shot back. "Even if it were another guy, I would think that he's innocent. He doesn't remember anything."

"So what? He's the one that did it. End of story."

Will turned around and walked down the hallway. Then he turned and entered his bedroom.

Jon pulled out a chair from under the dining table and sat down. He was not able to believe what he was going through. He had never been in a situation like that before. It was a hard choice. Although he thought Mike Riley was innocent, he was beginning to think that he *should* be put in jail. He did not want to let that out, though. He did not want his brother's words to get through him, even though they were starting to.

The following day, at the police station, Jon and Will decided to speak to Susan. They walked over to where she was. She was reading an article on how much people of different professions got paid a year.

"We need to tell you something," Jon started.

"Do you know what I have always been wondering?" Susan asked, interrupting Jon. "Why do superstars get paid more than police officers and firefighters and everything else that has to do with protecting? I mean, the superstars don't do anything but entertain people. On the other hand, officers protect people. Therefore, they protect the superstars. I've always wondered that."

"That's true," Jon stated. "Why *do* stars get paid more?"

"Officers should get paid more money."

"Yes, they should," said Jon. "Anyway, I need to tell you something."

"Yes?"

"We finally found out who the killer is. This time, it's the actual killer."

"That's great. He's arrested, right?"

"No, not yet."

Will then added a statement to what Jon had said. "But he's going to be arrested very soon."

"You'll never guess who it is," Jon told Susan.

"Who?"

"It's Mike."

Susan was shocked. "Mike?" she asked as she placed the article on a table. "How can he be a murderer?"

"If you've noticed that he's been acting very strange—especially when you ask him a question about his past—it's because he has no memory on it. Well, in his past, he was the killer."

"What?" Susan was astounded. "So what you're trying to say is that Mike was a murderer before and then he received memory loss and now he's who he is now?"

"Exactly. Do you think that he should be taken to jail?"

Susan thought about it for a moment. She then answered, "I think you should judge by how a person is on the inside and not on the outside."

"Oh, you're just like Jon," Will said sourly.

"I mean, inside he's a good person and he's not a killer, but on the outside he is. You're just judging a book by its cover."

"So that means if a killer just suddenly decided to be nice, you wouldn't take him to jail because of who is on the inside? Is that what you're trying to say?"

"No. I'm just saying that…" Susan could not finish. She was thinking that Will was right. Instead of arguing with him, she said, "We could put him on trial. It'll be the only way to determine if he's guilty or innocent."

"Now *that* I agree with," Will said, "because I know that he's going to be guilty." Then he walked away.

As Jon watched his brother walk away, he said, "I told him yesterday to wait a few days to arrest Mike."

"Did he agree with that?" questioned Susan.

"Miraculously, he did."

Jon then looked away and said, "This is awful. This is one of the worst situations I've ever been through."

"I can tell," Susan stated. "But you should take it out of your head because it's going to be all right. The best thing to do is to put him on trial."

"And what if Will's right? What if he's guilty? I think they're going to consider him guilty because there's no way for them to think that he is innocent. I'm like the only one that thinks that."

"Just don't worry too much about it, Jon. It'll be over before you know it. I have a feeling that everything's going to turn out right."

"I hope you're right." Jon then changed the subject. "Okay, let's get to work now."

While Will was on his way to the chief of police's office, he ran into Mike. He glared at him.

Mike looked back at him and said, "It's okay, Will. You don't have to worry about me. I'm out of here."

"Murderer," said Will. "You killed my father."

Mike sighed. "I can see that you're not going to take it lightly."

"You're going to jail as soon as possible. You're so lucky that my brother talked me into waiting a few days before you go. I don't even know what I'm waiting for."

Mike stayed silent.

"This was your way, huh? This was your way of hiding. You tricked us all. The killer was near us this whole time and we didn't know it. I should have known."

"Think whatever you want to think. *I* didn't kill your dad. The other me did it."

"Damn you, assassin. I hope you get the worst torture possible. I can't wait until you do."

"You're right. What are you waiting for?"

"Go to hell," Will said bitterly. Then he walked away towards the office of the chief of police.

Days had passed. It was two days before Mike was going to be arrested. That day was going to come quickly.

It was a cloudy day. The snow had fallen over the night and it left a smooth blanket on the ground. It was very deep and it made driving quite a problem. The streets obviously were cleared out first or else it would be almost impossible to drive.

People who were walking here and there were cold. It was freezing outside. The temperature was five degrees below zero. That was mostly the coldest part of the day—the morning. Then in the afternoon the temperature rose up a bit. At night, it dropped down again but it usually was not colder than the morning. Sometimes the night *was* the coldest part of the day.

The trees looked lifeless in the wintertime. It made it harder for deer to hide in the forest. Before it was easy for them to escape from predators by running off into the trees. Now it was harder since many of the leaves were gone and it was easier to see where they were running.

Nearby there was a frozen lake. A doe and its fawn were walking towards the icy lake. Their feet were buried deep in the snow and they were walking slowly and steadily. The fawn, with its curiosity, looked down at the frozen lake and put its right front leg over it. Then it stepped onto it and it began to slip and slide. The mother stepped onto the ice as well and went over to help her child, although it would be hard for her to walk on it as well.

Not far from that lake, Mike was in front of his cottage. He was shoveling up the snow so that the pathway would be cleared. He tried to clear everything out of his mind while he was doing that. He was not able to, though. Since he was thinking so much, he did not realize what he was doing. He stuck the shovel in the snow too deeply. It was already hitting the ground because the snow was not so deep anymore since he cleared most of it away. He kept on trying to shove the tool in but it kept on hitting the ground. Soon he *did* notice that there was not that much snow left and that he was hitting the ground.

"Man, I'm stupid," Mike said to himself. "I have to start being much more attentive."

While Mike continued to shovel up the rest of the snow, a car stopped by in front of the pathway. Susan stepped out of the car and shut the door. She walked down the cleared pathway and over to Mike.

Mike realized that Susan was there. He looked up at her for a moment. Then he continued shoveling and said, "Looks like everyone knows now, huh?"

"Yeah," answered Susan. "I guess you can say that."

"Will now hates me more than ever."

"That's the way he is. I guess because one of the people that the killer killed was his father.'

"I guess so."

Mike took two steps forward because he was done shoveling snow in that one part of the pathway. Now he had to move up and shovel more snow that was there.

"I'm moving into my new house tomorrow," said Mike. "This time it's for real. But I guess there's no point in moving into a new house since I'm going to be locked up."

"I'm sorry, Mike, but there's nothing else we can do. We're going to have to put you on trial. It's the only way."

"I know. I understand that. I'm just trying to say that there's no point in moving into a new house because I'm going to be found guilty and I'm going to go to prison."

Susan did not say anything.

Mike stopped shoveling. He looked up and continued to speak. "It's like moving into another country. You move there and like the place. Well, everything's going fine until some people say that you're going to jail. You don't know what for. You're totally confused but they say that you're guilty of something. That's how I feel. I still don't know why I'm going to jail."

"I know," Susan told him. "I know that that's what you're feeling but there's nothing that we can do about it. I wish we could, but we can't. Don't worry about it so much—maybe you'll be considered innocent."

"No," Mike answered as he shook his head. "That's not the way it works here. I know that they're going to keep me locked up for quite a long time—probably for life. I'll still be wondering why I'm there. I just wake up and start a completely new life. I thought that everything was going great. I got a job and I was going to live in a new house. Everything was fine. Now all of a sudden, I'm being blamed for something that *I* particularly didn't do. It was another person. I'm being arrested for something that another person was responsible of." He began to speak emotionally now. "You just don't know how it feels. It's not a good feeling."

Susan looked at Mike sympathetically. She began to feel sorry for him. She knew that he was dejected and she was beginning to feel that way as well. "I'm sorry, Mike," she said. Her voice was shaky when she spoke. "If it were up to me, I would find you innocent."

Mike shook his head slowly and dropped the shovel on the ground. "No, Susan," he said. "Don't say that. If it were some other guy in my place, you would consider him guilty. You know you would."

Susan gave Mike a hug. She knew that he was suffering a lot. She knew that he did not expect something like this to happen. She was starting to feel the sorrow that he had.

As Mike hugged Susan back, he smelled the scent of the perfume that she used. It reminded him of the way the beautiful fields smelled when it was not wintertime. It was a nice fragrance. He thought that he would never smell it again. All he would smell was the odor of the filthy prison cells. That was all.

Jon and Will were at their house. Jon was sitting at a table reading a few papers. He was thinking of different things at the same time.

Will came from the hallway and entered the living room. Then he went inside the kitchen. He opened the cabinet and pulled out a glass cup. He closed the cabinet and after that he opened the refrigerator and pulled out a gallon of water. He took the cap off and poured some water inside the cup. Then he put the gallon back inside the refrigerator and closed the door.

Jon stopped reading the papers. He set them down and said, "Mike retired."

Will took a drink from the cup and said nothing. He exited the kitchen and walked over to a couch and sat down.

Jon continued to speak. "You know, you remind me of when we were kids. You were always the same. I still remember that time when you got that dog for Christmas. Boy, did you love that dog. Every time you came home from school, the first thing you did was play with it. And then weeks later we got new neighbors. The man that was there looked over the fence days later and saw the dog. He hit it with his slingshot in the eye and blinded it. I saw the whole thing. When I told you, you got so angry. You wanted to kill that man. Well, the next day the man died in a car crash. You didn't care. You wanted to get his son now because you wanted to see one of the family members being tortured. You were bad. You're still the same way now."

Will finally spoke. "That was different," he started. "That wasn't right. I shouldn't have been like that. I don't know why you're saying that I'm still the same way now. That boy and that man were two totally different people."

"Mike and the past Mike are like two totally different people, too."

"No, they're not. They're the same person."

"With two completely different personalities!" Jon said angrily as he stood up abruptly from the chair. "I don't know what to say to you anymore. You see? I agree with some of the things that you say. I admit that you have a point in your part. But you always have to stick with what you say. You must always be right. Can't you at least find something right in what I think? No—of course not. That's just the way you are. Your way is always right. Everyone else is wrong to you."

"Are you trying to make me change my mind?" Will questioned. "Because if you are…"

"No, I'm not," Jon said more calmly now. "What I'm trying to say is that you don't see through other people's perspectives. I mean, maybe they have something right in their part, too. Like I said, I admit that you *do* have something right in your part. You have a point. I can't walk around either knowing that Mike killed our father. But despite that, I can't walk around knowing that Mike is in jail for a crime that *he* didn't commit. I mean he *now*."

Will said nothing and Jon sat down. He was calmer now. He wanted his brother to realize other people's opinions. He knew that Will had a right to have his own opinion but he was handling it too cruelly with Mike. Now that, he thought, was not right.

After Susan left, Mike went for a walk around the forest that was behind his house. He had nothing else better to do. He wanted everything to get out of his head anyway. He wanted to think of something other than what had been happening.

Soon Mike saw a snow rabbit hopping away from a coyote. The rabbit stopped shortly behind Mike's right leg. It was looking for a place to hide. The coyote was not far behind. It showed up moments later.

Mike bent down and picked the rabbit up. The rabbit did not even move. It knew that it was safe from the coyote. It just sat still.

Meanwhile, the coyote looked at the rabbit in Mike's hands. It was confused. It stood there for a moment. Then Mike scared it away. The coyote ran off into the trees and looked for something else to eat. Maybe something less elusive.

Mike took a few steps ahead. He looked at the rabbit for awhile. Then he placed it on the ground and let it go off. He had it continue its life as it was.

Later Mike found himself at the beautiful scene behind his cottage. He spotted the doctor sitting next to the lake. He walked over to him.

The doctor looked up and saw Mike standing next to him. "Nice view, isn't it?" he asked.

"Yeah," Mike answered as he crouched down next to the doctor. "This is the place I visit every time I need to feel better about things."

"That case is still bothering you, isn't it?"

"I don't want to talk about it. I'm trying to forget about it for now."

"Forget about it now, but you're going to remember about it again later on."

Mike stayed silent. He looked straight ahead. The sun was beginning to set over the land. It made everything look fiery orange. It was a nice view.

The doctor continued to speak. "So what's happened?"

Mike sighed. Then he spoke. "They're going to put me on trial."

"Really? Now that's an idea."

Mike glanced at him. "You would do the same thing?"

"If I had to, I would."

"I guess everybody would, wouldn't they? That's the only thing they *can* do because everyone's opinions are fluttering everywhere." He paused for a moment. "Anyway, what's *your* opinion about it?"

The doctor took a few moments to answer. "Have you ever thought about this? See? They're judging by how you were in the past because that was still you, right? Physically that was you, but mentally it wasn't. That doesn't matter to them anyway. *But* if you were a very good-hearted person back then and an evil person now, they would judge by how you are now and not in the past. Don't you find that rather odd?"

"I understand what you're trying to say."

"The only thing that matters is the evil that you have done in your life. It doesn't matter how good you were or are to them."

"So, in your opinion, do you think I'm innocent or guilty?"

"To me, neither. There's actually no way you could be either one. I know it's strange."

"What do you think the judges will say?"

"If they were to stick their minds on the present and stop living in the past, then you know what they would say. If they think that the past is always living with them, then their thoughts would be different. It's all a matter of opinion anyway. I really can't predict what they will say."

Mike stood up. "It's been nice talking to you, doc."

"Where are you going?" questioned the doctor without looking at him.

"Home, I guess."

"Why are you leaving so soon?"

"It's getting dark."

"Why don't you sit back down? This may be the last time that we speak to each other. You're leaving tomorrow, aren't you?"

"Yeah."

Mike sat back down. He lifted his knees a few inches from his chest and put his arms around them. He grabbed his left wrist with his right hand. Then he said, "Thanks, doctor."

"For what, Mr. Riley?" the doctor asked with confusion.

"I don't know—for everything. I would probably be lost by now if you never picked me up when I was lying on the ground. I would probably never have found my home because I don't think that I would have picked up the suitcase that was next to me. I would have possibly thought that it belonged to someone else. So thanks for helping me."

"Mr. Riley, it was my job. I couldn't have left you lying there."

"What if it wasn't your job? Would you still have helped me?"

"Honestly, yes I would have. I would have checked to see if you were alive first. And if you were, I would have taken you to a nearby hospital."

"How many people these days would have actually done that?"

"Not many, Mr. Riley. Not many."

"I know. I've seen people walk by others that are suffering from a broken leg or that have just been shot. People just take a look to see what's going on and then they keep on walking by. Well, of course they'd do that. Many people these days act as if they're suffering so that they are able to draw the attention of a certain someone and later kill that person.

"I was lucky to get a person that knew what he was doing. Yeah, there are some complications in this life I'm living but if you never had showed up, then who knows where I would be right now? I would probably be in a worst situation than what I'm facing now."

"You are a very strong young man, Mr. Riley."

"Yeah, well, I'm trying not to be *too* strong."

It was silent for a moment. Mike then said, "Well, I'll see you around, doc. It's really getting late."

"Farewell, Mr. Riley. Until next time."

Mike extended his arm and shook the doctor's hand. "Thanks again," he said.

The doctor smiled. "You're welcome."

Then Mike stood up and turned around. He walked away into the dark trees. He stepped over a log and as soon as he did, he heard the sound of an animal scurrying away. He looked down to see what it was, but he saw nothing. He continued to walk. Many branches were hanging down and blocking his path. He moved them out of the way and stepped over more logs.

It was very eerie walking through the trees in the dark. There was absolutely no light whatsoever. There were too many trees and their branches and leaves were blocking the moonlight. It was pitch-black. Mike had to feel the branches on his face in order to move them out of the way. He also had to crash into a log to know that it was on the ground. He seriously was not able to see anything but darkness.

Mike heard the crickets chirping and many other animals making strange noises. It was quite an experience going through the forest in the night.

Minutes later, Mike finally saw a shaft of moonlight. There was a small gap between the trees, so the light went through that gap.

Mike walked through the light and continued walking through the forest. It was back to darkness again. The wind began to blow and there was a nice sound when it began to blow through the trees.

Soon Mike was out of the forest. He was able to see again. It felt as if he had been blind while he was walking through the trees. Now he was able to see the cottage that he was going to sleep in for one more night. He walked over to it and pulled out his key from his pocket. He unlocked the door and opened it. He stepped inside the house and closed the door behind him.

Mike grabbed a bag and pulled out a pair of scissors. He walked down the hallway and into his bedroom. He grabbed the dark coat that he used to wear in his past life. Then he began to cut it. It was difficult to shear the fabric, but the more he kept trying, the easier it was. He continued to cut it until it was not possible to wear it anymore.

After Mike was done destroying the coat, he grabbed the pieces and threw them out. He wanted to be sure that they would never be found ever again.

It was the day for Mike to move to his new house. He already had his furniture taken there. Now all he had to do was travel there. The way to travel there was by foot.

Mike arrived at the house an hour later. He looked at the exterior. It was beautifully painted white and red. The windows were crystal clear. The fence was polished and painted light brown. It was a nice place to live in. It was also peaceful. The only difference from the previous place in which Mike lived was that there were neighbors.

Mike entered the house and dropped his things off inside. He took a walk around the place. The tile was clean and nice. The living room was behind the kitchen. In the living room, there was a hallway. There were four rooms in the hallway. They were bigger than the cottage's rooms.

Mike thought that the house was perfect for him to live in. He said to himself, "I don't even know why I moved in such a nice place. I'm not going to stay here long anyway."

After taking a tour around the house, Mike looked at the backyard. The grass was green and there was a tree on the upper left corner. Many flowers were growing sporadically and there was a pool. It was also very pleasant.

Mike then went back to the front yard. He looked around. He knew that if he were not going to go to jail, he would be very content living there.

Soon a man that lived on the left side of the house shouted, "You my new neighbor?"

Mike turned to him. "Yeah," he shouted back.

"Nice place, huh?"

"Yeah, it's pretty nice."

The man looked at the driveway. "No car?"

"No. I'm planning on getting one later—much later."

"I just moved in a few months ago. No one's lived in that house until now."

"Really?"

"Yeah."

"Well, I'm not going to be staying here for long."

"Why?"

"Many reasons why. You'll find out tomorrow."

The man was silent for a moment. He broke his silence. "You living alone?"

"Yeah."

"So am I. It's nice and peaceful."

"Yeah. I've lived alone all my life. Well, as long as I can remember."

"Wow. Where'd you used to live?"

"In a cottage in the middle of the forest."

The man laughed. "What? That's outrageous. Why'd you live there? No money?"

"Yeah, I guess so. It was nice there, though."

"You ever had any bears stop by?"

"No, but I've encountered upon one before."

"What'd you do—run?"

"No. It needed help, so I helped it. Then it left. I've gotten along with many of the animals that lived in the forest."

"Wow. That must have been neat. If I lived there, I would have been dead meat by now."

Mike had no response for that. He just said, "Well, it was nice talking to you. I'm going to go inside now."

"Okay," said the man. "Bye. I'll talk to you later."

"Yeah," Mike responded as he turned around and walked toward the front door of his home. "If you're able to."

It was late at night. Mike was in his bedroom, lying on his bed and staring at the ceiling. He began to think of everything. "Tomorrow's the day," he said to himself. "Tomorrow's the day that I'm going to be gone."

Mike sat up in the bed and looked out the window and through the window that belonged to the neighbor on the right side of the house. He saw a woman putting her child to bed. She covered it up with a soft and white blanket. Then she turned to her older son and said goodnight to him. It was very obvious.

Mike stopped looking out the window. He lied down again and thought that the family next door was lucky that they had a family. Little did they know what it was like to be without a family. It was lonely and horrible. There was no one there for you when you needed problems. There was no one there to comfort you. It was hard.

The next day came. Mike hardly did anything that day because he knew that there was nothing to do. It would be worthless to do anything. All he did was prepare himself for anything that was going to happen. He knew that they were coming for him.

It was around ten o'clock at night. Mike was outside his house. He heard the sound of cars coming. Soon two police cars showed up. Jon and Will stepped out of one. Susan stepped out of the other.

All Mike did was look at them. He knew that his time was coming.

"I'm sorry, Mike," Jon said as he began to walk towards Mike.

The man that lived on the left side of Mike stepped out of his house. "What's going on?" he asked. "Why are you guys arresting him? He didn't do anything."

"It's a long story," Mike answered lowly as he looked at the man. He knew that the man was able to hear him.

The man was shocked.

The man that lived across the street looked out his window. He gasped. "It's him," he said as he watched everything going on.

Mike walked closer to the police cars. Susan walked over to him and said, "We have to do this. We don't want to, though."

"I know," Mike answered.

Soon the man that lived on the left side of Mike yelled, "Look out!"

Susan looked and said, "Mike, get out of the way!"

At the same time, the man that lived across the street yelled at the officers, "Watch out!"

Mike was turning around, but he was shot in the back and as he turned around, he was shot twice in the chest. He fell to the ground.

The man that lived across the street had shot him. "Is everyone all right?" he asked.

Susan yelled and ran over to Mike and kneeled beside him. She looked at the man and shouted, "Why did you do this?"

"He's a killer," said the man. "He killed the woman that lived in the house he's living in."

"But he's not a killer anymore," said Jon. "He got amnesia."

The man's jaw dropped. "I'm sorry," he said. "I didn't know."

Susan looked down at Mike and began to cry. "Please, Mike," she said. "Hold strong. Don't go away. Please."

Mike looked at her. "At least we don't have to worry about me being innocent or guilty anymore, right? At least Will doesn't have to walk around knowing that I killed his father, but knowing that they killed me."

After those words, Mike was gone.

Susan looked down at the floor and cried more. "No," she said. "Why? Why did this have to happen?"

Jon was not able to believe what was happening. He walked over to Will and said, "There. You happy now?" After that, he walked towards the police car.

Will watched him as he walked away. Then he looked over at Mike's body. His expression showed that he, too, was shocked. He did not expect anything like that to happen. Although he wanted

Mike to be tortured, he felt bad. He somehow had a change of heart and knew that Mike was a good person and did not deserve to die at that moment.

The man that lived next door now understood. He was in total dazedness. He stood there and watched everything.

The man that lived across the street was shocked as well. He thought that he did the right thing. He thought that he was protecting everyone because he thought that Mike was still a killer. But unfortunately he was not.

The man slowly turned around. He leisurely began walking toward his house. Once more he looked back at Mike. Then he continued to drag his feet toward the front door. While he was walking he dropped the gun onto the ground.

0-595-27202-9